FINDING ANSWERS

L. A. DOBBS

CHAPTER ONE

The farmhouse door was ajar, a jagged slice of blackness cutting through the snow-bright day.

Jo Harris froze behind the wheel of her truck, her breath fogging the glass. Garvin McDaniels was a stickler for order. Doors shut, paths shoveled, lights on when the sun went down. But now, the front steps were buried under a fresh layer of snow, untouched, the house eerily dark.

Something wasn't right.

She climbed out, her boots crunching on the driveway as the cold bit through her coat. The air was unnervingly still, thick with the kind of silence that makes you question every sound you didn't hear.

Garvin wasn't just Jo's landlord. Lately, she and her sister had been softening him up with casseroles, hoping he'd sell them the cottage. But it wasn't only that—Jo liked him. He was lonely, and their talks had become something she looked forward to. Which made the open door and eerie silence all the more unsettling.

Jo's hand hovered near the holstered weapon on her hip as she grabbed the casserole dish from the passenger seat.

Her pulse kicked up as she climbed the snow-covered steps, her eyes fixed on that gaping door.

"Garvin?" she called, her voice cutting the stillness like a blade.

No answer.

Jo's grip tightened on the dish as she nudged the door open wider and stepped into the shadows.

The smell slammed into her—sharp, metallic, and unmistakable.

Blood.

Inside, the farmhouse was a wreck. Chairs over-turned, glass scattered across the floor like glittering shards. Jo's pulse quickened as her eyes tracked the dark stain smeared across the hardwood. A path of destruction led to the living room. To the body.

Garvin McDaniels lay in the middle of it, sprawled across the floor, eyes wide open. Cold. Lifeless.

Jo's stomach dropped. "Garvin!" Her voice

cracked in the silence as she rushed forward. She didn't even realize she'd tossed the casserole onto the table.

She dropped to her knees next to him, pressing her fingers to his neck, searching for a pulse. His skin was like ice. The faint metallic scent in the air confirmed what her mind was trying to deny.

No pulse. No life.

Jo pulled back, trying to steady her breath, her hand trembling. It wasn't the first body she'd seen in her career. But Garvin... Garvin was supposed to be alive. He didn't deserve this kind of death.

She fumbled for her phone, hands still shaking. "Reese," she managed when the receptionist picked up. "Garvin's dead. I found him here, at his house. Send the team. Fast."

Reese's voice crackled with shock. "Jo? Are you okay? What happened?"

Jo swallowed hard, her gaze flicking to the blood-stain spreading beneath Garvin. "It's bad. It looks like... murder."

"I'm sending everyone. Ambulance and the team are on their way. Stay put."

"Okay." Jo hung up and exhaled, the air thick and tainted with blood. Her fingers curled into fists as she fought for control. She should be handling this better.

She was trained for this. But this... This was different.

Her mind raced, trying to piece together the scene, to make sense of the chaos. Garvin had been reluctant to sell the cottage at first. But after months of coaxing, he'd seemed to come around. Just last week, he'd told her he was almost ready to sign.

Now, he was dead. Why?

A knot tightened in her chest. Did his death have something to do with the property? Jo glanced at the open door, the wind blowing in snow that melted on the blood-streaked floor.

She needed answers.

The distant wail of sirens cut through the silence, snapping Jo back to the present. Her pulse steadied. Time to get to work.

She scanned the room again, this time with the sharp focus of a cop at a crime scene. The overturned chair near the table. A broken lamp. Glass scattered like stars across the hardwood. Every object out of place told part of a story, and Jo was determined to piece it together.

Her gaze landed on Garvin's body, the pool of blood that had already begun to congeal. She crouched again, eyes narrowing as she took in the angle of his limbs, the way his head rested against the leg of the overturned coffee table. He'd been hit with something heavy, but there was no sign of a weapon.

The door was forced, so the killer had broken in, and it must have been sometime before the last snowfall earlier that morning.

She took out her phone and snapped photos. Kevin, one of the deputies, would do this later for the police photos, but Jo knew that every broken item, every smudge on the floor, every piece of disturbed furniture—they all mattered. She'd need them later.

The sirens stopped abruptly as the first responders arrived, a flurry of voices and boots heading toward the porch. Jo rose, stepping back as the crew began spilling into the house. But her eyes never left the room. The details were still sharp in her mind, each one locked away.

She took a deep breath, the icy air burning her lungs. Garvin deserved answers. And she'd make sure he got them.

THE WHITE ROCK police Tahoe and the old Crown Victoria pulled up, tires crunching on the snow. Sam, Wyatt, Kevin, and Lucy piled out, urgency etched on their faces.

Lucy bounded up the steps, her nose twitching, already working the scene. Jo crouched, scratching the German Shepherd behind the ears for a quick second, grounding herself.

"What's the situation?" Chief Sam Mason asked, stepping into the doorway.

"Busted lock. Struggle inside," Jo said, her voice clipped, professional, though the sight of Garvin still twisted her gut.

Inside, the team moved fast. Wyatt snapped photos, his face grim. Kevin, already gloved up, began collecting evidence, his hands moving with the precision of a surgeon.

"Anything missing?" Wyatt called from the living room, camera still in hand.

Jo's eyes swept the room. Everything looked as cluttered as usual, and everything was in its place— except for one thing.

"Wait." Her voice sharpened as she stepped toward the shelf by the window. "Garvin had a bronze sculpture here. Of an elk. His great-uncle made it. He thought it was valuable."

Wyatt joined her, eyes narrowing as he studied the empty shelf. "Valuable enough to kill over?"

Jo's gut tightened. "Maybe."

Sam, standing near the door, gave a quick nod to

Wyatt and Kevin. "Check the other rooms. See if anything else is out of place."

They moved through the house in sync. Jo stood still for a moment, taking in the scene, her mind ticking. Garvin didn't have much. A couple of antiques, some knickknacks, but nothing anyone would risk breaking in for.

Wyatt reappeared from the hallway, shaking his head. "Nothing. Bedrooms, bathroom—all untouched."

Kevin followed, glancing around. "Doesn't feel like a burglary. Just the one thing missing? That doesn't track."

"What else would the motive be?" Sam asked.

"Maybe someone didn't like him." Kevin nodded toward Garvin's battered face. "I mean, sure looks that way."

"Or something he was about to do," Jo said, suspicion creeping into her voice. "Garvin was about to sell me the cottage I've been renting. Remember?"

Sam raised an eyebrow. "Yeah, and when he was dragging his feet, you started bribing him with pie and casseroles." His tone was light, and for the first time that morning, Jo smiled.

She glanced at the table, where she'd stashed the latest casserole, now sitting cold and untouched. She'd started looking forward to those meals. "It worked.

Last time I was here, he said he was almost ready to sell."

Kevin, sifting through broken glass, didn't look up. "Wasn't someone else interested in buying it?"

Jo nodded. "Yeah, but Garvin told me he didn't trust them. He wanted the property to go to the right person, said he thought that person was me."

Wyatt chimed in, "Did you get anything in writing?"

Jo shook her head. "No, nothing official yet."

Wyatt sighed, wiping a hand across his jaw. "That means the other buyer could still be in play. If it's just your word, they'll have a chance."

"His heirs will be in charge of it now anyway," Sam said, looking down at Garvin. He shook his head.

Jo frowned, unsure. "I doubt the other person wanted the property bad enough to kill him to stop him from selling to me. That would be crazy."

But even she wasn't convinced. Not anymore.

"Maybe the bust is more valuable than we know." Sam said.

Wyatt frowned, scanning the room. "Could be they knew exactly what they wanted and went straight for it."

Sam folded his arms, glancing at the broken lock. "But why not just break in and take the bust? Why kill Garvin?" His eyes shifted to Garvin's lifeless body.

"Maybe they thought he wasn't home and he surprised them?" Kevin suggested.

Before anyone could respond, Lucy began whining, pawing at the floor beside the body. Kevin noticed, raising an eyebrow.

"I think she wants us to roll him," he said.

Sam nodded. "ME's on the way, but go ahead. Carefully."

Jo crouched as they turned Garvin onto his side. The back of his head revealed a second wound, deep, matted with blood. The floor beneath him was stained dark red. But that wasn't what had Lucy's attention.

Nestled beneath the body was a small, coiled piece of plastic. A hair tie.

"What's that?" Wyatt crouched down, squinting at it.

Jo's hand went reflexively to her own head, fingers brushing against the familiar spiral holding her hair in a tight ponytail. Her brow furrowed.

Sam, always sharp, caught the movement. "Could it be yours? Maybe it fell off when you found him?"

Jo stiffened. "No, it's not mine. It's still on."

Sam's gaze lingered on her for a second longer than she liked. "Could've been here from a past visit.

Maybe you didn't notice. In which case it really wouldn't be evidence."

Jo's jaw clenched. Was he serious? Was he offering to look the other way? Like it wasn't worth bagging?

Kevin glanced between them, waiting. Jo met Sam's gaze, the weight of the moment heavy between them. Did he think she had something to do with this, or was he trying to protect her from being unjustly accused? Didn't matter either way—the hair tie was not hers.

"No," Jo said, her voice firm. "It's not mine. I'm sure of it. I'd know if it fell out. Let's bag it and run the hairs."

Sam raised an eyebrow, a flicker of something—doubt? concern?—in his eyes. He gave a quick nod to Kevin. "Bag it."

Kevin picked up the tie carefully, holding it up to the light. "Two curly hairs."

Jo's stomach twisted. "They're not mine."

Sam's voice was calm, measured. "Of course not." But the look he shot her said more than his words. He nodded at Kevin. "Bag it and tag it."

The boards on the porch creaked as Medical Examiner John Dudley arrived, his gait slow and steady. The team shifted, giving him space. Lucy wagged her tail at the sight of him, momentarily breaking the tension.

John set to work, his face impassive as he examined the body.

Sam stepped back, glancing at his team. "All right, folks. ME's in charge here. Let's head back to the station, start processing. The sooner we get this evidence logged, the closer we are to figuring this out."

CHAPTER TWO

The heavy glass door of the old post office creaked as Jo pushed it open. The White Rock Police Station smelled of brewed coffee and worn wood, a comforting mix that always made her feel like she was stepping into the past. The reception area, with its brass post office boxes and scratched pine floors, was warm and homey. At least for a police station.

Reese was on her feet before Jo crossed the threshold. Her big blue eyes filled with concern. "You okay?"

"Yeah, I'm good," Jo said, keeping her voice steady, though her insides hadn't caught up yet.

Reese wasn't buying it. "Bridget said you were getting close to him." Her tone softened, like she didn't want to spook Jo.

Jo nodded, keeping her expression unreadable. Liking someone didn't guarantee they stuck around.

She walked past Reese into the squad room. Major, the station's black cat, sat perched on a filing cabinet, watching the room like he owned it. Lucy trotted over to Jo, and Major leaned down to sniff the dog, blinking slowly and deliberately, as if passing judgment on the dog.

Jo went straight to the Keurig, her hands working on autopilot, setting up coffee for the team. The motions kept her busy, kept her mind from unraveling.

"Garvin have next of kin?" Sam's voice cut through the air. He stood by the window, his face in shadow. His tone wasn't casual. He was already thinking ahead, turning something over in his mind.

"He's got two kids, but they're not local," Jo replied, focusing on the sound of the coffee brewing, anything to steady herself.

Kevin chimed in. "I'll track them down."

Sam gave a curt nod. "Wyatt, check his financials. See if there's anything off."

Wyatt was already at his keyboard, typing fast, eyes narrowed. The guy worked like he had something to prove.

"Reese," Sam continued, "download the photos. Get them printed. I want them on the board." He paused, glancing at Jo. "And see if you can find a value on that bronze bust. Jo can fill you in."

Jo passed out the coffees, watching Sam out of the corner of her eye. He wasn't saying everything, but that was typical. There was something lurking behind his eyes, something he wasn't ready to share yet.

The door swung open, and Marnie Wilson strode in, her heels clicking on the worn floor. Jo's gaze snapped to her, and that feeling in her gut stirred. Marnie looked too concerned, her perfectly composed face a little too tight.

"Is it true? Garvin McDaniels is dead?" Marnie's voice wavered, but there was something behind it that Jo couldn't place. Something that didn't sit right.

Sam watched her closely, his eyes narrowing. "News travels fast," he said, voice measured. "Were you close to him?"

Marnie blinked, too quickly. "Well, no, not close. But I spoke to him a few times. You know, I wanted to understand what seniors in town care about. It's part of my campaign."

Jo's stomach twisted. There it was—Marnie's politician mask slipping back into place. Jo didn't trust her. Never had.

"What happened? Was it a heart attack? A

stroke?" Marnie pressed, her fingers curling tight around the strap of her bag.

Sam didn't miss a beat. "Can't comment on an ongoing investigation," he said, voice cool.

Marnie paled. "An investigation? You mean he was murdered?" Her voice jumped, but there was something in her eyes that Jo caught—fear, maybe. Or something else.

"Like I said," Sam replied, his tone unchanged, "we can't comment."

Marnie took a breath, smoothing her skirt with a practiced hand. The veneer of concern fell back into place. "Of course. It's just... It's always upsetting to see one of our fine townspeople pass away."

Her words were polished, perfect for a campaign, but Jo wasn't buying it. Jo watched Marnie walk out the door, her gut telling her this wasn't merely concern for a local's passing. There was more to it. A lot more.

CHAPTER THREE

S am stood in front of the corkboard in his office, eyes scanning the crime scene photos, each one a piece of a puzzle he couldn't quite solve. Jo leaned against the desk, arms crossed, the weight of Garvin's death pressing heavily on her.

"All right," Sam said, low and measured. "Let's go over the scene."

Wyatt and Kevin exchanged a glance, the tension in the room thick. Lucy dozed in a patch of sunlight by the window, oblivious.

Jo stepped forward, eyes locked on the picture of Garvin's body. "They broke in, surprised him."

Sam nodded, brow furrowed. "But why? What were they after?"

Wyatt pointed to a shot of a smashed chair and

scattered dishes. "He fought back. Not bad for a guy his age."

"Yeah, but whoever it was, they won," Kevin added. "One person? Or more?"

Sam turned back to the board, narrowing his eyes at the chaos. "Hard to say. The snow covered any footprints. But this seems more like a beating than a robbery."

They all stared at the photos for a few beats.

Kevin broke the silence. "I went back after John left. Dusted for prints."

"And?" Sam asked without looking away from the board.

"Only found two sets."

"Garvin's, for sure," Sam said, turning to face the team.

Jo shifted, her stomach tightening. "And mine."

Wyatt cleared his throat, tapping his fingers on the desk. "So all we've got is the hair tie unless we find some DNA somewhere else in the house?"

Kevin tapped a pen against his notepad. "Lab's running DNA on the hairs. We'll have something in a few days."

Sam's eyes flicked to Jo. There was something in his look—concern, maybe, or suspicion. "We need to dig deeper into Garvin's life. His finances, his relationships. There's a motive here, buried under the surface."

Jo bit the inside of her cheek, thinking about the last few times she'd talked with Garvin. She hadn't seen any trouble on the horizon, but maybe she had missed something.

"Anyone else think Marnie's visit was strange?" Sam asked, his voice tight.

Jo straightened. "Yeah, especially since Garvin mentioned her as one of the buyers for the cottage."

Sam frowned. "Right. You said that before."

The room went quiet, the implications hanging in the air.

Wyatt broke the silence. "You don't think Marnie killed him?"

Sam shook his head. "Wouldn't be her style."

Kevin snorted. "Can't see her getting her hands dirty."

Sam's jaw tightened. "Still puts her on the list."

Wyatt leaned forward. "She seemed eager to know what happened. Like she was fishing for information."

"Or making sure we didn't have any," Kevin added, suspicion edging his voice.

Sam's eyes stayed on the board. "I'll handle Marnie. We need to be careful. She's too connected in this town."

Jo's fingers drummed against her arm. "What about Garvin's kids? Any luck finding them?"

Kevin flipped through his notepad. "Got their contact info. Both out of state—one in California, the other in Florida. I have calls in to them."

Sam nodded. "Good. What else?"

Wyatt cleared his throat. "I'm still digging into Garvin's financials. So far, nothing suspicious."

Jo pushed off from the desk, pacing. "We need to check with his neighbors too. See if anyone noticed anything unusual."

"Agreed." Sam made a note. "Here's the plan—DNA results are pending. I'll handle Marnie. Kevin, you're on the kids and neighbors. Wyatt, keep at the financials. Jo, you get with Reese and see if you can figure out what that bronze statue was worth."

CHAPTER FOUR

Jo sat down next to Reese at the reception desk, an old green metal relic from the station's earlier days as a post office. Major stretched lazily on the corner of the desk, eyeing them with casual disinterest. Lucy, always alert, sat by Jo's feet, her tail occasionally thumping against the floor.

Reese glanced up from her computer, curiosity written all over her face. "So, tell me about this statue. What exactly did it look like?"

Jo leaned back, thinking. "It was a bronze elk. Tall, regal. Standing in grass. Garvin always said it had been in his family forever, but I don't remember who made it. He was proud of it, though."

Reese nodded, her fingers already tapping at the

keyboard. "All right, bronze elk. We'll see what we can dig up."

Major hopped off the desk and sauntered over to Lucy, rubbing against her as if to remind the German Shepherd who was boss. Lucy sniffed him and then laid her head back down.

Jo smiled slightly, watching the interaction. It wasn't that long ago that they were archenemies. Now, they seemed to be coexisting peacefully.

"Bridget's coming by later," Reese added. "She's bringing something from the bakery. Probably those almond croissants you like."

Jo's smile grew at the mention of her sister. Bridget landing that bakery job had been a godsend. "She's doing great there. I'm really happy she's found something she enjoys. It's a good fit."

Reese grinned. "She's a natural. And hey, I'm definitely not complaining about all the free treats."

Jo chuckled softly, feeling a little lighter for the first time in hours. Major leaped back up onto the desk, settling beside the keyboard as Reese clicked through images on the screen. Jo's attention shifted back to the search.

"Okay, let's see if any of these look familiar," Reese said as they scrolled through pictures of bronze sculptures. Some were close, but none quite matched the one from Garvin's place.

Lucy whined softly, sensing Jo's lingering tension. Jo reached down, giving her a quick pat. "None of these feel right," Jo muttered, frustration bubbling up.

They continued searching, Reese typing the keys around Major's tail, which kept making its way onto the keyboard. Jo's eyes caught on an image. She leaned in, heart quickening. "Wait—that one. That's it."

Reese clicked on the image, bringing up the details. The bronze elk stood tall and proud, its legs rooted in a patch of grass, like the one she remembered at Garvin's.

Reese scanned the description. "Stanley Clifton, huh. It says here it's a hundred years old. Clifton's stuff is valuable—really valuable."

Jo frowned. "Clifton... Garvin mentioned his great-uncle made the statue, but I don't remember hearing the name Clifton. Could Garvin have been related to him?"

Reese tapped the screen. "Maybe. Stanley Clifton was apparently a big deal. His original works go for high tens of thousands."

Jo's gut tightened as the implications hit her. "So if Garvin's bust was an original, we're talking pretty good money."

"Exactly." Reese sat back, glancing at Jo. "But it also says that there are replicas that only go for about a hundred."

Jo exhaled slowly, trying to piece things together. "Garvin wasn't flashy. He wasn't the kind of guy to brag about his stuff, but he did always say that statue was special. Maybe he didn't even know how much it was worth... if it even is the original."

Reese clicked through more details about Clifton's work. "We need to figure out if Garvin's bust was the real deal. If it was a Clifton original, we're probably looking at a planned theft, not just some random break-in."

Jo nodded. "That changes things. This wasn't just about taking something off a shelf. Someone knew what they were after."

Reese raised an eyebrow. "You think Garvin's family would know? Any chance they could tell us if it's been passed down?"

"Maybe. We'll have to find out."

Lucy's ears perked up two seconds before Sam walked into the area. Lucy immediately went over to stand beside Sam, who gave her a quick pat on the head before looking at Jo and Reese.

"I'm heading over to Marnie's campaign office,"

Sam said, his tone casual but focused. "Figured Lucy could use some air."

Jo and Reese exchanged a knowing glance, rolling their eyes in unison. Jo leaned back in her chair. "You want me to come along?"

Sam shrugged, a faint smirk tugging at the corner of his mouth. "Maybe I'll get more out of her going in solo."

Reese snorted softly. "Oh, you'll get something out of her, all right. But be careful—Marnie's after more than information."

Jo chuckled under her breath. There was no love lost between her and Marnie, and she didn't mind not accompanying Sam.

"Did you guys find out anything about the statue?"

Jo told him what they had found, and Sam nodded thoughtfully.

"So maybe this was about money, then," he said.

"Maybe."

"But if so, why was Marnie so interested? Do you think she truly was concerned about a town resident?" Sam asked.

Reese snorted.

Sam smiled. "Lucy and I will do our best to find out."

With that, he gave Lucy's leash a light tug, and they headed toward the door. Jo watched him go, a small grin still on her face as she turned back to the screen. "Good luck with that."

CHAPTER FIVE

Marnie's campaign headquarters buzzed with activity as Sam pushed open the glass door, Lucy padding silently beside him. The sharp scent of fresh paint hung in the air, mingling with coffee. Volunteers huddled over computers, pinning flyers on corkboards. It was a scene of organized chaos.

Something in the back caught Lucy's attention. She trotted off, nose twitching, as she made her way toward the far wall, where a new campaign sign was being painted. Sam's eyes followed her—and that was when he saw him. Desmond Griggs. The town thug, barely out of his teens but already making a name for himself.

What was he doing here?

Sam frowned. He hadn't thought Desmond cared

about politics. But then again, maybe it wasn't politics he was here for.

At the center of it all stood Marnie, honey-blond hair catching the overhead light. She was all smiles, gesturing to her team like a natural, drawing them in. Sam paused, watching her. The charm was undeniable—but so was the undercurrent of something darker.

Marnie's eyes found him across the room, and her smile widened. She excused herself from her staff and strode over, heels clicking on the polished floor.

"Sam," she greeted him, her voice warm but with a touch of flirtation. "Twice in one day? I must be lucky."

"Something like that," Sam said, unmoved. "I need a word. In private."

Something flickered across her face—concern, maybe, but gone before he could be sure. Lucy joined them as she led him to a small office off the main room, shutting the door behind them. Lucy sniffed along the edges, her nose twitching.

Marnie gestured to a chair. "Please, have a seat."

Sam stayed standing. His eyes scanned the cluttered desk—papers, campaign flyers, a wall covered in polling data. "Thanks for making time, Marnie. I know you're busy."

"Always time for you, Sam." She perched on the edge of her desk. "What can I help you with?"

"I wanted to follow up on your visit to the station. You seemed pretty concerned about Garvin McDaniels."

Her expression shifted to one of civic duty, brows knitting just enough. "Of course. Garvin was well respected. His loss is a tragedy for the community."

"Right," Sam said, his tone neutral. "How well did you know him?"

She hesitated, barely a second. "I told you, I spoke with him about senior initiatives. It's an important part of my platform."

Sam took a step forward, eyes narrowing. "There's talk you were interested in buying some property he owned. A cottage."

Her smile faltered. "What? I didn't realize Garvin had a property for sale."

Sam tilted his head, watching her. "Not officially. But I heard you asked about it."

Marnie's voice tightened a fraction. "I've been focused on my campaign, Sam. I wouldn't waste my time with a cottage. There's too much at stake right now."

He didn't blink. "You sure? You seemed upset at the station."

Marnie straightened, arms crossing over her chest. "As the future mayor, I care about everyone in this town."

Sam glanced out through the office's glass wall, catching sight of Desmond Griggs lingering in the back. His mouth tightened. "Even Desmond Griggs?"

Marnie followed his gaze but didn't flinch. "Of course. I know he's been in trouble, but he's turning things around. I'm giving him a chance."

Sam studied her, wondering if she believed that—or if she just wanted him to believe it. He wished Jo were here. She could read people better than he ever could. If Marnie was really helping Griggs, maybe she wasn't as bad as they thought.

"All right, Marnie," Sam said slowly, letting the weight of the conversation settle. "Thanks for your time. I may need to talk to you again."

"Of course." The relief in her voice was palpable. "Anything to help. You know where to find me."

Sam nodded and turned toward the door, Lucy trotting at his side. But as he left, something gnawed at him. Jo had said Garvin told her that Marnie was interested in the property. Marnie said no. One of them was lying—and it wasn't Jo.

So the question was, was the liar Marnie or Garvin?

CHAPTER SIX

Jo was at her desk, trying to untangle Garvin's family tree to link him to Stanley Clifton, when the door banged open. She looked up as her sister, Bridget, burst in—an anxious whirlwind of energy—along with the sweet smell of freshly baked cookies.

"Jo!" Bridget called, clutching a white bakery box to her chest, apron still dusted with flour. "I heard about Garvin. Are you okay?"

Jo pushed back her chair, scraping the worn floorboards. "I'm fine, Bridge," she said, standing as Bridget wrapped her in a tight hug. The scent of vanilla and cinnamon clung to her clothes.

Bridget pulled back, her eyes scanning Jo's face. "I

can't believe it. Garvin... Who would want to hurt him?"

Jo shook her head, her voice low. "That's what we're trying to figure out."

Wyatt and Kevin had been hovering nearby, and Bridget noticed them for the first time. She lifted the bakery box. "I brought cookies. I didn't know what else to do. I just... needed to bring something."

Kevin stepped forward, taking the box. "Thanks, Bridget. We could use something sweet about now."

The group gathered around Jo's desk, opening the box to the smell of warm chocolate chip cookies.

Bridget glanced around then lowered her voice. "What happened? Can you talk about it?"

Jo sighed, running a hand through her hair. "Someone broke into his house. There was a struggle..."

Her words trailed off, the image of Garvin's body flashing in her mind. Wyatt picked up where she had left off, his tone flat. "Could've been a robbery gone wrong. But it sure felt personal."

Bridget's eyes widened, her hand flying to her mouth. "Oh, God. Poor Garvin."

Jo reached over, squeezing her sister's hand.

Silence fell over the group, broken only by the soft crunch of cookies. Bridget scanned the room, her brow furrowing. "Where's Lucy? I brought her a special treat."

"With Sam," Kevin said, brushing cookie crumbs from his shirt. "He's talking to Marnie Wilson."

Bridget's eyebrows shot up. "Marnie Wilson? The woman running for mayor? What does she have to do with Garvin?"

Jo and Wyatt exchanged a look before Jo spoke. "Not sure yet. Sam's just following up on something."

As if on cue, a loud meow echoed through the station. Major sauntered over, his green eyes locking on to Bridget like he owned the place. He stopped in front of her, his gaze expectant.

Bridget smiled, reaching into her apron pocket. "I guess Lucy will have to wait for her treat. You want it, Major?"

The cat meowed again, more insistently. Bridget placed a small dog treat on the floor, and Major snatched it up, trotting off like he'd just caught dinner.

Bridget watched him go, her brows drawing together in confusion. "Where's he going with that?"

Jo smirked, leaning back in her chair. "Not sure. He's got a spot somewhere he's burying them."

Kevin chuckled. "Probably hiding them from Lucy. Smart cat."

Bridget paused, her hands resting on the edge of the

table. "I guess I'll have some extra time on my hands now." She glanced at Jo with a small smile. "Maybe I can find someone else who appreciates home-cooked meals."

Jo grinned. "Well, that frees you up to cook more stuff for us."

Bridget laughed softly, but as she said it, her eyes flickered briefly to Kevin, who was reaching for another cookie. He caught her gaze and quickly looked away, a faint blush creeping up his neck.

Bridget checked her watch and stood. "I'd better get back to work. My break's almost over."

Kevin stood as well, grabbing his jacket. "I'll walk out with you. I'm on my way to talk to Garvin's neighbors, see if they noticed anything suspicious."

KEVIN HELD the door for Bridget as they stepped out into the parking lot, the winter sun bright but offering little warmth. They both tugged their jackets tighter against the cold.

"So, how's the new job?" Kevin asked as they walked toward his car. He was using his own today since Sam was out with the Tahoe.

Bridget's face lit up. "Oh, I love it. The bakery is

great—smelling fresh bread and pastries all day, regular customers... It's helping me feel like part of the community."

Kevin smiled, genuinely glad for her. "Sounds perfect."

They paused by the cars, neither in a hurry to leave. Kevin hesitated. "You doing okay? Haven't noticed anything... strange?"

Bridget's smile faltered just for a second. "I'm fine. But... I still look over my shoulder a lot."

Kevin's heart sank a little. Bridget had shared parts of her past with him, stuff she didn't talk about with others. It meant something that she trusted him.

"Keep your eyes open," Kevin said quietly, glancing around the empty lot.

"I will," Bridget assured him, her smile returning. She changed the subject. "Any progress on that thumb drive thing?"

Kevin stiffened. The thumb drive. It had been haunting him since he found it, tucked in with his things after the hospital. The data on it pointed to an old narcotics case and had led them to the burial grounds of a serial killer. But the way he'd retrieved the password—he couldn't tell Sam or Jo about that. Not without blowing his cover. And he was sure there was more to the thumb drive than they'd discovered thus far.

"Not much to report," he said, trying to keep his tone light.

Bridget gave him a look, her brow furrowing. "You still have it, right?"

"Yeah." Kevin glanced around again, instinctively checking the lot. They were alone, but he still felt like someone was watching. "I'll be glad when it's all over. I need to clear the air with Sam and Jo."

Bridget hesitated then smiled softly. "I could help, you know. Maybe take a look with you? Sometimes, a fresh pair of eyes spots things."

Kevin felt a warmth spread through him. "That'd be great. You sure?"

"Of course." She grinned. "Besides, I've got to find someone to feed my casseroles to now that Garvin's gone."

Kevin chuckled, nodding. "Thursday night?"

"Sounds good." Bridget winked. "I'll bring the food. You bring the mystery."

"Sounds like a plan."

"I'll walk back to the bakery from here. It's just a block away," she said, pointing down the street. She gave him a quick wave before heading down the sidewalk, disappearing around the corner. Kevin watched her go, feeling a strange mix of relief and tension settle over him.

As he headed toward his car, something caught his eye—a folded piece of paper tucked under his windshield wiper. His easy mood vanished. He slowed, frowning.

He yanked the paper free, unfolding it carefully. The words, scrawled in thick black ink, made his blood run cold.

BE *careful what you dig for.*

KEVIN'S PULSE QUICKENED. He scanned the parking lot, eyes darting from car to car, but the place was empty. Too empty. The winter sun, bright just moments ago, seemed harsh now, casting long shadows that stretched across the asphalt.

He crumpled the note in his fist, heart racing. His mind spun with questions, but one thought echoed louder than the rest.

Someone knows.

Kevin shoved the note into his pocket, his hands trembling as he reached for his car door. He quickly slid into the driver's seat, locking the doors behind him.

For a moment, he just sat there, staring straight ahead, his breathing shallow.

Who else knows about the thumb drive?

He started the engine, his thoughts racing as fast as his heartbeat. He couldn't shake the feeling that he had crossed into dangerous territory—territory where someone was watching his every move.

As he pulled out of the parking lot, that sense of unease stuck with him, heavier now. Whatever this was, he was in deeper than he'd ever imagined.

And someone was making sure he knew it.

CHAPTER SEVEN

Later that afternoon, Jo hadn't made any progress tying Garvin to Stanley Clifton when Sam returned with Lucy, her tail wagging as she padded into the station. Jo noticed a streak of blue on her tail.

"Lucy, what did you get into?" Jo asked, crouching down to inspect it.

Sam chuckled, shaking his head. "Marnie's volunteers were painting campaign posters. And guess who was there?"

"Who?" Jo asked, though she already had a sinking feeling she knew the answer.

"Desmond Griggs." Sam's voice carried a note of disdain.

Jo's eyebrows shot up. "Griggs? Really? What's she thinking?"

Sam shrugged. "She says she's giving him a chance."

Jo snorted, reaching for a pair of scissors from Wyatt's desk. "Good luck to her. He's more likely to burn her campaign down than help it." She carefully snipped the painted fur from Lucy's tail. "Any luck with Marnie?"

Sam shook his head, running a hand through his salt-and-pepper hair. "She's sticking to her story. Says she was never interested in the property."

Jo snorted. "Sure, because pushy's her style."

Wyatt glanced up from his computer. "So Marnie's lying?"

"Seems like it." Sam nodded. "Or Garvin was. But why lie? What's so special about that land?"

Jo's mind raced, recalling her conversations with Garvin. Something about the way he had talked about the property stuck with her. "He told me he didn't trust her—said she was too aggressive."

Sam frowned. "Think he could've been confused about who else was interested?"

"Doubt it. He was sharp." Jo paused, the puzzle pieces still not fitting together. "He mentioned something about the land having 'potential,' but I thought he meant the view. What if it's something else?"

"Like what?" Wyatt leaned forward, interest sparking in his eyes.

"I don't know. But whatever it is, it's enough for Marnie to lie."

The room fell silent as the implications hung in the air. Jo could almost see Sam turning the information over in his head, trying to make sense of it.

Wyatt broke the silence. "You really think she'd kill for it? She's running for mayor."

Sam met his gaze. "And since when have politicians been squeaky clean?"

Wyatt smirked. "Fair point."

Jo crossed her arms. "Marnie wouldn't be the first official involved in something shady. Might not even be the first one to kill."

Sam nodded, a flicker of determination in his eyes. "All right. Wyatt, I want you to follow her. See what she's up to after she leaves her campaign office."

Wyatt was already grabbing his jacket. "You got it. I'll keep it low-key."

Sam sighed. "I've gotta call Garvin's son and daughter. Not calls I'm looking forward to."

Jo winced. "I don't envy you."

Sam glanced at the clock on the wall. "Might need a drink at Holy Spirits after that. You in?"

Jo smiled. "I could be persuaded."

The soft click of nails on hardwood interrupted the moment. Lucy, who had been dozing in the corner, was suddenly alert. She sniffed the air, padding over to the filing cabinet with growing interest.

"What is it, girl?" Jo asked, watching as Lucy's tail wagged with excitement.

Lucy pawed at the base of the cabinet, whining softly. Jo knelt down, curious. Her fingers brushed against something small and hard. Pulling it out, she found a bone-shaped treat—the one Bridget had given to Major earlier.

"Well, would you look at that," Jo said, holding it up.

Major sauntered into the room, his green eyes narrowing at the sight of Lucy nosing around his stash. The black cat's tail twitched with irritation.

"Sorry, Major. Looks like your secret's out." Jo tossed the treat to Lucy, who caught it mid-air with a crunch. Major's look of disdain was almost comical as he turned and leapt onto a nearby desk, his back to them.

Wyatt zipped up his jacket, laughing. "Looks like it's almost quitting time. I'll get a jump on following Marnie, see what she's up to after the campaign HQ."

Jo nodded. "Let me know if she does anything worth raising an eyebrow."

Wyatt flashed a grin. "You know I will."

As he headed out, Jo's mind raced. What was so special about the property? She'd lived in that cottage for years—nice spot, sure, but nothing worth killing over. But Garvin had hinted at something more. Something about the land.

Was Marnie lying about wanting it?

Was Garvin's death about the land or the valuable bronze statue?

Two possible motives and no time to waste figuring out which one was real. If Garvin had died over a piece of land or a bronze elk, it didn't matter—they had to find out fast.

Jo glanced at the clock. Every second counted.

CHAPTER EIGHT

Jo pushed open the heavy oak door of Holy Spirits. The bar still held the soul of the decommissioned church it had once been—dim stained glass windows cast slants of red and gold across the floor, and worn pews had been refitted as booths. The altar, stripped of its old role, now served as a bar, rows of liquor bottles lined up like offerings.

The familiar scent of whiskey and polished wood wrapped around Jo like a worn blanket. She slid onto a stool near the bar, drumming her fingers on the scarred wood. "The usual, Pete."

Pete, a burly man with graying hair and a colorful tattoo on his forearm, poured her drink without a word, setting it down with a slight nod. Jo took a long sip, savoring the burn. Garvin's lifeless face flashed through her mind, followed by Marnie's too-slick smile at the station. Something wasn't adding up.

The door creaked, and Sam entered, broad shoulders silhouetted against the dying light from outside. His gaze found her immediately, and Jo gave a quick nod. He made his way over, settling beside her on a stool.

"Rough day," Sam said, ordering a beer. It wasn't a question.

Jo swirled the whiskey in her glass. "You could say that."

Pete returned with Sam's beer, and they sat in silence for a beat, the low murmur of conversation around them blending with the faint strains of classic rock from the jukebox.

"Talked to Garvin's kids," Sam finally said, breaking the silence. "They're flying out tonight and agreed to come to the station tomorrow."

Jo's grip tightened on her glass. "And what do you really make of Marnie saying she never wanted to buy the property?"

Sam shrugged. "Maybe Garvin was confused."

"You don't buy that," Jo said, looking at him squarely. "She barged into the station, practically demanding information. That wasn't just *neighborly concern*."

Sam's jaw clenched, a tell she knew well. "Politicians are good at lying, Jo. We can't go accusing her without proof."

Jo opened her mouth to argue, but the words faded as the door opened again, and Mick Gervasi sauntered in. Dressed in his usual black leather, the private investigator scanned the room with practiced ease before his gaze settled on them. Mick had known Sam since they were kids, and he'd helped them on a case or two when things got murky.

"Hey, Mick." Sam gestured to the empty stool on Jo's other side. "Perfect timing."

Mick slid onto the stool, waving to Pete. "Whiskey on the rocks," he said then turned to Sam and Jo with a grin. "What's got you two looking like somebody died?"

Jo gave a dry laugh. "Somebody did."

Sam gave Mick a rundown on Garvin's death and Marnie's suspicious behavior. "She's denying any interest in his property, but Jo's certain Garvin mentioned her."

"Definitely did," Jo said, her voice hard. "So why lie? What's special about that property?"

Mick's eyes narrowed as he thought it over. "Isn't she tangled up with Convale?"

"No, that's Beryl Thorne," Sam said, frowning.

"But Convale's pumped a lot of money into Marnie's campaign."

Jo looked up, her interest piqued. "That's right. I'd forgotten about that."

Mick took a slow sip of his drink, ice clinking in the glass. "Want me to dig around? See what shakes loose?"

Sam nodded. "Wouldn't hurt. Jo's got a gut feeling, and it's usually on point."

Mick leaned in, voice low. "You know, speaking of Convale, my prior research dug up some rumors of an exposé a few decades ago. Journalist dug into Convale's dealings but never published. Rumor is someone paid to keep it quiet."

Jo and Sam exchanged a look. "Think it's connected?" Jo asked.

Mick shrugged. "Maybe not. But my gut says there's something there."

Sam shook his head. "Doesn't seem tied to Garvin's death, but..." He trailed off, clearly thinking it over.

Jo sipped her whiskey and glanced around. A few regulars sat in booths along the far wall, hunched over drinks, and the occasional laugh or muttered conversation drifted through the space. Jo looked around, the familiar faces adding to the warmth of the bar despite the shadows in her mind.

Mick swirled his ice, breaking the quiet. "What about the Webster case? Feds finally packed up?"

Sam's expression darkened. "Yeah, they're done at Hazel's place. Ricky's there alone now."

Jo shook her head. "Poor kid. He's been through enough."

"Hazel's great-niece is raising hell, saying Hazel was framed," Sam said, lowering his voice.

Jo raised an eyebrow. "Framed? After what they found?"

"Some people can't face the truth," Mick muttered.

A silence fell over them, each lost in thought. Jo's mind wandered to her sister, missing for years. The old ache sharpened, familiar and raw.

Mick caught her expression. "They never found her, did they?"

Jo shook her head, unable to speak for a moment. Finally, she managed, "No. Which means..."

"Hazel might have another dump site," Sam finished, his jaw clenched.

The weight of it settled over them, heavy and dark. Jo took another long sip of whiskey, letting it burn away the chill.

"We'll keep looking, Jo," Sam said, his hand briefly touching her arm. "We won't give up."

Jo nodded, grateful for the support. But the dread gnawed at her. The Webster case, Garvin's murder, Marnie's lies, Convale's money—everything felt tangled, pieces of a larger puzzle she couldn't see.

"One thing at a time," Mick said, reading her thoughts. "We'll start with Marnie and Convale. See where it leads."

Jo managed a nod, feeling a flicker of relief. "Thanks for helping."

They sat in silence, finishing their drinks, each lost in thought. The flickering light from a candle on the bar cast long shadows over them, blurring edges, hinting at secrets hidden in White Rock's past.

Jo's instincts told her one thing—nothing here was ever simple, and with every step they took, something darker loomed.

CHAPTER NINE

B ridget poured hot water over a tea bag, the steam curling into the small kitchen. The scent of chamomile filled the air, soothing, but her fingers froze on the handle as she heard the crunch of gravel. Jo's truck had pulled up, and a familiar prickle of worry stirred in Bridget's chest. She grabbed a second mug, dropped in another tea bag, and went to the door.

Through the window, she saw Jo crouched by the steps, hunched shoulders barely visible in the evening light. Bridget's stomach tightened. Jo looked worn, her tired eyes focused on Pickles, the orange tabby who'd made himself part of their porch. Usually wary of anyone getting too close, Pickles leaned into Jo's hand as if sensing her weariness.

"Hey," Bridget said softly, stepping out with two steaming mugs.

Jo glanced up, a tired smile on her face. "Hey, sis."

Bridget set the mugs on the railing and crouched down beside her, reaching out to stroke the cat's back. "Would you look at that," she murmured, stroking the tabby's soft fur. "Guess he's warming up to us."

Jo nodded, her hand slowing. "Yeah, maybe he'll even come inside one of these days."

"At least he's got the porch," Bridget said, offering Jo her tea.

Jo took the mug, her face tightening as she blew on the tea. "Bridge, we need to talk about the cottage."

A chill went through Bridget that had nothing to do with the temperature. "What about it?"

"Garvin's kids are flying in tomorrow. With him gone..." Jo trailed off, glancing at the cat curled up at her feet.

Bridget's throat felt dry. "They might not want to sell to us."

Jo nodded, her gaze drifting. "We don't know what they'll decide."

Bridget gripped her mug, fighting to steady her thoughts. This place had become her sanctuary, her first real taste of stability in years. The thought of losing it, of being uprooted again, left her feeling untethered. She gestured to Pickles. "And him? If we have to leave..."

Jo reached over, squeezing her arm. "Hey, let's not get ahead of ourselves. We'll figure it out."

Bridget forced herself to nod, swallowing against the knot in her throat. *You just got settled here. Don't let it slip away.*

She shivered as a gust of icy wind swept through the trees, rustling the last of the fallen leaves across the gravel. She tugged her sweater tighter, glancing at Jo. "Let's head inside before we freeze."

Jo nodded, giving Pickles one final pet, then led the way. They stepped into the cottage, a cozy warmth washing over them. Though she'd only recently moved in, the place already felt like home to Bridget. Jo's "cottage chic" style filled every corner: thrifted knick-knacks, well-loved furniture, and stacks of books. Jo had spent years scouring yard sales, picking out pieces with the same care she put into everything.

Bridget took it all in, grateful for the warmth and familiarity. The glow of a table lamp cast a soft light over the overstuffed couch, the polished wood floor, and the shelves lined with a mix of Jo's true-crime novels and her own well-worn self-help guides.

In the corner, their goldfish, Finn, swam up to the side of his aquarium, seemingly undisturbed by the chill they'd left behind. Outside, the soft trickling of the stream running through the woods added to the cottage's peaceful hum. Bridget set her mug down, taking in the small details that made the place feel whole.

Jo moved to Finn's aquarium, sprinkling in a flake of food. The goldfish darted up, snapping it in an instant.

"At least someone's happy to see me," she muttered, a faint smile crossing her face.

Bridget leaned against the doorframe, studying her sister's face. "Any leads on Garvin?"

Jo's smile faded. "Not yet. But it was violent, Bridge. Someone killed him, and I can't shake the feeling it's tied to this property."

A chill settled over Bridget as she glanced at the window, the shadows outside feeling deeper, closer. Her hand twitched, her mind flashing to the gun hidden under her bed. She hadn't told Jo about it—or about everything else she'd tried to leave behind. Jo had saved her, pulled her out of that life, given her a chance at something better. If Jo knew the whole truth, would she still look at her the same way?

Instead, she forced a bright smile. "I brought home some bread from the bakery. They were about to toss it. I could warm it up, make some olive oil and balsamic?"

Jo's face softened. "Sounds great."

Bridget busied herself in the kitchen, grateful for the distraction. She sliced the bread with careful precision, her hands steady despite her swirling thoughts. She didn't have to tell her sister everything. Not yet.

As she arranged the bread on a plate, her eyes drifted to Jo, sitting by the fire, her gaze distant. One word, and it could all unravel. Her past felt like a shadow that stretched over everything, threatening the life she'd built here, the peace she'd barely begun to trust.

She brought the bread to the table, trying to focus on the simple comfort of food and warmth. Jo looked up as Bridget set down the plate, a flicker of gratitude in her eyes.

"Thanks," Jo murmured. She took a slice, dipping it in the oil, savoring the simple meal as if it were a feast.

Bridget took a seat across from her, her own slice of bread in hand. The fire crackled softly, casting a warm glow over the room. It was quiet, peaceful—everything she'd ever wanted.

As she looked around, Bridget realized just how

fragile it all was. A missing landlord. A violent death. A past that refused to stay buried. She tightened her grip on the bread, her mind racing with what-ifs. But she didn't have to face them alone. Not here, not with Jo beside her.

Jo caught her gaze, a small, reassuring smile softening her face. "Whatever happens, we're in this together."

Bridget nodded, her own smile wavering but determined. "Together."

CHAPTER TEN

The next morning, Sam stood as Derek and Leanne McDaniels entered his office, their faces drawn with grief and something else—tension, maybe even fear. He gestured to the chairs across from his desk.

"Thank you for coming," Sam said, his voice low and respectful. "I'm sorry for your loss."

Derek nodded stiffly while Leanne murmured a quiet "Thank you." They sat, shoulders rigid, eyes darting around the room.

Sam leaned forward, hands clasped on his desk. "I know this is difficult, but I need to ask you both some questions about your father."

"Of course," Derek said, his voice rough. "Anything to help find who did this."

Sam nodded, studying their faces. "When was the last time you spoke with your father?"

Leanne answered first, her voice barely above a whisper. "Three days ago. He called us both."

"Together?" Sam asked, raising an eyebrow.

Derek shook his head. "No, separately. He... He had some news for us."

Sam waited, sensing there was more to come. After a moment of tense silence, Leanne continued.

"Dad told us he was planning to change his will," she said, her eyes fixed on her hands in her lap. "He wanted to leave both his properties to some environmental trust instead of us."

Sam's eyebrows shot up. "Both? Including the cottage?"

Derek nodded, his jaw clenched. "All of it. Said he wanted to 'protect the land' or something. He'd been talking like that for months, getting more paranoid about the property."

"Did he say why?" Sam asked, leaning forward.

Leanne shook her head. "Just kept saying there were people who wanted to ruin the land and wanted to preserve it. We thought he was being dramatic, or maybe..." She trailed off, glancing at her brother.

"We wondered if he might be getting senile,"

Derek finished, his voice hard. "Turns out he was serious."

Sam nodded slowly, processing the information. "Did he say who these people were?"

Leanne and Derek shook their heads.

"And the will hadn't been changed yet?" Sam asked.

"No," Derek confirmed. "He was meeting with his lawyer this week to finalize it."

The implications hung heavy in the air. Sam kept his face neutral as he asked, "And how did you both feel about this change?"

The siblings exchanged a look. "We were shocked, of course," Leanne said carefully. "Hurt, even. But it was Dad's property to do with as he wished."

Derek snorted, earning a sharp look from his sister. "What?" he snapped. "Are we pretending we were fine with it? That land's been in our family for generations. It should have stayed that way."

Sam watched the interplay between them, noting every reaction. "I understand this must be difficult," he said. "Just a few more questions. Where were you both the night your father was killed?"

Derek straightened in his chair, his face a mask of indignation. "Are you seriously asking us for alibis? We're his children, for God's sake!"

Leanne placed a calming hand on her brother's arm. "Derek, please. I'm sure it's just standard procedure." She turned to Sam, her eyes wide. "I was at home in Boston. I had a Zoom call with my book club until about ten p.m. Several people can verify that."

Sam nodded, jotting down notes. "And you, Derek?"

Derek's jaw clenched. "I was at a bar with colleagues. We were celebrating landing a new client." He pulled out his phone, tapping furiously. "I've got receipts, time-stamped photos, whatever you need."

"You can't seriously think we had anything to do with this," Leanne said, her voice trembling. "He was our father."

Sam held up a placating hand. "I assure you, this is standard procedure. We have to rule out every possibility, no matter how unlikely." He paused, bracing for their reaction to his next request. "I'll also need to get your fingerprints and DNA samples."

"What?" Derek exploded, half rising from his chair. "This is outrageous! We came here to help, not to be treated like criminals!"

Leanne tugged at her brother's sleeve, urging him to sit back down. "Derek, please. Let's just cooperate and get this over with." She turned to Sam, her face pale but composed. "Of course, Chief Mason. Whatever you need."

Derek sank back into his chair, glaring at Sam. "Fine. But I want it on record that we're only agreeing to this under protest."

Sam nodded, keeping his expression neutral. "Duly noted. I appreciate your cooperation. It's crucial in helping us find who did this to your father."

As he led them to the processing room for fingerprinting and DNA collection, Sam couldn't shake the feeling that there was much more to this story. The changed will, the secrets Garvin thought needed protection, the tension between the siblings—they all pointed to a motive far deeper than he'd initially suspected.

JO LOOKED up from her paperwork as Sam emerged from his office, Garvin's children in tow. She watched as he handed them off to Reese for processing, her eyes narrowing slightly at the tension visible in their shoulders.

Sam caught her gaze and gave a subtle nod. After years of working together, Jo could read volumes in that small gesture. Something about the siblings didn't add up.

As Reese led Derek and Leanne away, Sam made his way over to Jo's desk, perching on the edge with a sigh.

"So?" Jo prompted, keeping her voice low.

Sam ran a hand through his hair. "Garvin was planning to change his will," he said, his tone measured. "Wanted to leave the entire property to some environmental trust instead of the kids."

Jo's eyebrows shot up. "The whole property? Including my cottage?"

Sam nodded. "Apparently. But here's the kicker—he hadn't finalized it yet. Was supposed to meet with his lawyer this week."

"Let me guess," Jo said, leaning back in her chair. "Bruce Benedict?"

"Got it in one," Sam confirmed. "We'll pay him a visit, see what he knows."

Jo nodded, her mind already racing with the implications. "The kids can't have been happy about the change."

"Understatement of the year," Sam muttered. He glanced around the office then lowered his voice further. "Listen, something's off with those two. I can feel it."

Jo watched as Sam stood and casually made his way over to Wyatt's desk. She couldn't hear what was said, but she saw Sam slip Wyatt a piece of paper, speaking in low tones. Wyatt nodded, his face serious as he immediately turned to his computer.

Sam returned to Jo's desk. "I've asked Wyatt to dig into Derek and Leanne. Phone records, recent travel, anything that might tell us if they've been in town lately."

"Good call," Jo agreed. She hesitated then asked, "Any word on Marnie?"

Sam shook his head. "Wyatt tailed her for a few hours last night. Said it was mind-numbingly boring. She went home and stayed there."

Jo frowned. "That seems... too easy."

"My thoughts exactly," Sam said.

Reese strode in, her normally cheerful face creased with a mix of exasperation and determination. "Derek and Leanne are processed and gone," she announced, her tone clipped.

Jo looked up from her desk, noticing the slight furrow in Reese's brow. "Everything okay, Reese?"

Reese sighed, holding up a small, colorful packet. "Look what I found in the supply closet, buried behind a stack of printer paper. Again." She shook her head, clearly annoyed at the disruption to her orderly domain.

Sam leaned back in his chair, a knowing look crossing his face. "Let me guess. Another one of Major's secret stashes?"

"Exactly," Reese confirmed, her eyes scanning the room for the culprit. "I swear, that cat thinks he's running some kind of underground treat operation in my supply closet."

As if summoned by the mention of his name, Major stretched atop the filing cabinet, his green eyes laser focused on the treat in Reese's hand. His tail swished back and forth with barely contained anticipation, one paw stretching out demandingly.

Lucy, who had been dozing near Jo's desk, lifted her head, suddenly alert to the possibility of snacks.

Jo shot the German Shepherd a warning look. "Don't even think about it, girl. That's definitely not for you."

Reese, despite her annoyance, couldn't resist Major's silent plea. She took a treat out of the little bag and tossed it onto the top of the cabinet. The cat stopped it from sliding off with surprising dexterity and immediately settled down to enjoy his prize.

"I don't know how he keeps getting into the treat

drawer," Reese muttered, straightening a stack of papers on her desk.

"Sorry, Reese," Sam said, though his amused tone suggested he found the whole situation more entertaining than problematic. "We'll try to keep a closer eye on his treat-hiding activities."

Reese nodded then seemed to remember something. Her face brightened slightly. "Oh, there is some actual case-related news. The lab results came back on that hair tie we found at the crime scene. There were roots attached to the hairs."

The atmosphere in the room shifted, all attention now on Reese.

"That's great," Jo said, leaning forward. "Any matches?"

"I'm running it through CODIS now," Reese replied, her efficiency shining through despite her earlier frustration. "It could take a while to get a hit, if we get one at all. But it's a solid lead."

Sam nodded, standing up. "Good work, Reese. Keep us posted on that. Jo, Lucy, and I are heading out to talk to Bruce Benedict about Garvin's will. Let us know immediately if anything comes up with those DNA results."

At the mention of an outing, Lucy's ears perked up, but her eyes remained fixed on Major, who was making a show of enjoying his treat atop the filing cabinet.

"Come on, Lucy," Sam called, grabbing his jacket. "Time to go."

Lucy whined softly, clearly torn between her duty and the possibility of Major dropping some crumbs.

Sam sighed, a hint of a smile on his face. "All right, how about this? We'll swing by Brewed Awakening. I think they just got a fresh batch of those doughnut holes you love."

The magic words "doughnut holes" had Lucy on her feet in an instant, suddenly the picture of a dutiful police dog ready for action.

Jo chuckled, reaching for her own jacket. "Well, that did it. Let's go see what Bruce has to say about Garvin's sudden change of heart."

As they headed for the door, Reese called after them, "I'll let you know as soon as we get anything on those DNA results. And Sam?"

He turned back.

"Maybe we should think about getting a lock for that treat drawer."

Sam nodded, his expression a mix of amusement and resignation. "Add it to the budget request, Reese. Though something tells me Major would find a way around that too."

CHAPTER ELEVEN

The law offices of Benedict & Associates occupied a stately Victorian on Elm Street, complete with gingerbread trim and a wraparound porch. Jo eyed the building as Sam pulled the cruiser to a stop, wondering how many of White Rock's secrets were locked away behind those heavy oak doors.

Lucy's tail thumped against the back seat, nose pressed to the window. Sam glanced at her in the rearview mirror, grinning. "This is it, girl."

"She'll think you're taking her for treats," Jo said, giving Lucy a quick scratch before stepping out of the cruiser.

The squeak of the porch steps brought Bruce

Benedict, tall and silver haired, to the door. His gaze softened when he noticed Lucy.

"Chief Mason, Sergeant Harris. It's been a while," Bruce greeted them, his usual warmth tinged with worry. His eyes landed on the dog. "And who's this beauty?"

Sam gave Lucy a gentle pat. "This is Lucy, our police K-9. She's one of the team."

Bruce nodded approvingly, scratching Lucy behind the ears. "Well, she's a fine-looking officer," he said with a small smile before waving them inside.

The office smelled of polished wood and old leather, an atmosphere that somehow suited Bruce. Jo settled into one of the leather chairs in his office, surrounded by walls of legal tomes and a desk that seemed too big for any one person.

"Thank you for seeing us on such short notice, Mr. Benedict," Sam began, leaning forward.

Bruce nodded, taking a seat behind his desk. "I'm glad to help. Garvin was more than a client—he was a friend. This has shaken the whole town."

"We're trying to make sense of everything," Jo said, choosing her words carefully. "We know Garvin had been thinking about changing his will."

Bruce's expression sobered. "He had, but it was

still up in the air. Garvin talked about wanting to leave a legacy, something that would protect the land."

"Protect it how?" Sam asked.

Bruce sighed, flipping through a file on his desk. "He wanted to prevent development on his property, make sure it stayed wild, untouched. We discussed him leaving it to a preservation committee instead of his kids."

Jo's eyebrows lifted slightly. "Did he give a reason?"

"Not directly," Bruce replied, his gaze thoughtful. "But he hinted at wanting to 'preserve something for future generations.' Said he didn't want his land turned into 'some developer's playground.'"

Jo's mind turned to Marnie's recent interest in the land. "So the will wasn't finalized?"

Bruce shook his head. "No, he wanted to sort out a few things before making a final decision."

"Like what?" Sam asked, his eyes narrowing.

Bruce closed the file and clasped his hands, looking uncertain. "One of the properties—on River Road. Garvin was debating whether to sell it before he signed anything. He had an interested party that he knew would take care of it and just wanted to be sure he was making the right decision."

Jo's heart lifted. River Road. Her cottage. Garvin really *was* going to sell to her.

"Did he mention who he might sell to?" Sam's voice was steady, but his gaze was sharp.

"No," Bruce replied, shaking his head. "He only said he was doing some research."

Jo leaned forward, her curiosity piqued. "Research? About what?"

"It was odd." Bruce's eyes took on a distant look, as if recalling Garvin's exact words. "He kept talking about the history of the land. He mentioned... old rumors. Said he wanted to 'verify some things' before he made any decisions."

"Rumors?" Jo repeated. "Did he say what kind?"

Bruce shook his head, looking frustrated. "No, but he was unusually cryptic. That wasn't like him. It was as if he'd discovered something he didn't trust."

Sam exchanged a loaded look with Jo. "And did he say who he might have been talking to about all this?"

"No names," Bruce said, drumming his fingers on the desk. "But he did mention meeting someone soon. Said it was important."

Lucy, who had been lying patiently by Jo's side, pressed her head against Jo's leg as if sensing the tension. Jo reached down, her fingers absently scratching Lucy's ears.

Bruce took a deep breath, his gaze drifting to the window. "He was really determined to do this right, to make sure the land wasn't just another piece of real estate. That was the last time I talked to him."

Jo shifted in her seat, processing. "So he didn't fully trust whatever information he had yet?"

Bruce nodded. "Exactly. I got the feeling there was something he hadn't told me. He was always straight-forward with his wishes—until recently."

Sam glanced at Jo, his brows furrowing. "Bruce, would there be any records here at the firm—anything that might show what he was researching?"

Bruce shook his head. "Garvin kept most of his personal documents close to the chest. He only brought in what we needed to update the will. So any additional information would likely be in his own files or with... whoever he was planning to meet."

Jo's mind was whirring, piecing together a picture that felt more sinister by the minute. Marnie's denial, Convale's donations, and Garvin's cautious approach. The land on River Road wasn't just real estate. To Garvin, it had become something worth protecting.

She caught Sam's eye, and he gave a small nod. He sensed it too—this wasn't just about family estates or preservation societies.

"Thank you, Bruce," Sam said, standing. "You've been a big help."

Bruce rose, showing them to the door. "Chief, Sergeant"—his gaze softened on Lucy—"and Lucy. I hope you find who did this."

"We're going to try," Jo replied, her voice a little tight. "Thanks again, Mr. Benedict."

As they stepped outside, a gust of cold air hit them, and Jo took a long, deep breath.

Sam was quiet as they made their way to the cruiser then finally muttered, "You thinking what I'm thinking?"

Jo's jaw tightened as she glanced back at the old Victorian. "I think Garvin knew something about that land. And somebody didn't want it getting out."

CHAPTER TWELVE

S am steered the cruiser into the drive-through lane at Brewed Awakening, rolling up to the speaker, where Zoe's cheerful voice came through loud and clear.

"Welcome to Brewed Awakening! What can I get for you today?"

Sam leaned out the window. "Hey, Zoe. Two coffees, the usual. And a box of doughnuts for the station." He glanced at the back seat. "And doughnut holes for Lucy."

Zoe laughed. "As if I'd forget Lucy's order. That dog has a memory like a bank vault."

Lucy gave a soft woof, pressing her nose to the glass, tail wagging.

"See that?" Jo asked, smiling. "She knows."

They pulled up to the window, and Zoe leaned out with their order. She handed Sam a tray with the coffees, a big box of doughnuts, and a smaller bag for Lucy. "Here you go, Chief. And Lucy, there's your special delivery."

"Thanks, Zoe," Jo said, taking the treats and passing the bag to Lucy, who carefully pulled out a doughnut hole, crunching it with satisfaction.

"You two look serious," Zoe said, eyeing them as Sam passed the tray to Jo. "Everything okay?"

Sam gave her a polite smile. "Nothing a little coffee can't fix."

They pulled out, the cruiser filling up with the smell of coffee and sugar. Lucy nosed the bag, looking for seconds, but Jo gently tucked it aside.

"Save some for later, girl," Jo said.

They drove a few miles in silence before Jo spoke up. "So... about the cottage."

Sam's eyes flicked toward her, his tone easy but direct. "You're worried about losing it?"

Jo nodded, tightening her grip on the coffee cup. "It's not just a place to live, Sam. It's home. For me, for Bridget, even for Pickles. Losing it would be..." She trailed off, shaking her head. "Not an option."

Sam gave a small nod. "If Garvin didn't finalize his

will, that leaves his kids in charge, right? And neither of them lives in White Rock?"

Jo's lips curved into a hint of a smile. "Exactly. They might be open to selling."

They stopped at a red light, and Sam glanced at her. "But?"

She sighed, her gaze drifting to the storefronts of White Rock sliding past. "But there's still that other interested party. What if they don't want me to be the buyer?"

"Marnie?" Sam's voice hardened. "Convale?"

Jo shrugged. "Could be anyone with a stake in this. They see something in that property Garvin never talked about."

Sam's jaw tightened. "We'll deal with that if we have to. Right now, let's stick to what we know."

The light turned green, and they moved forward. Jo found herself staring out the window, thinking of Bridget, Pickles, the garden Bridget had been dreaming up. She'd carved out a life here. Losing it wouldn't just be moving houses; it would be uprooting her entire peace of mind.

"You know," Sam said, breaking into her thoughts, "whatever happens, you've got people in your corner. Bridget, the team, and me. We're here."

Jo gave a quick nod, her smile small but genuine. "Good to know, Sam."

SAM PULLED the cruiser into the parking lot, the old post office-turned-police station coming into view. The familiar sight should've been reassuring, but Jo's mind was elsewhere—on Garvin, the will, and what it all meant for her cottage.

Reese was at her desk in the reception area, busy with the latest small-town issue.

"No, Mrs. Deardorff, the police department doesn't handle goat-related property disputes," Reese said, her voice a mix of patience and amusement. "Maybe you could talk to your neighbor about Bitsy's taste for petunias?"

Sam raised an eyebrow at Jo, a faint smile on his face. Some things in White Rock never changed. He stepped inside, the scent of doughnuts wafting ahead of him.

Reese's eyes lit up as she spotted the doughnut box. She mouthed a quick "Thank you" as she reached for a glazed twist, finishing her call with Mrs. Deardorff before turning to them.

In the squad room, Kevin and Wyatt perked up at

the sight of the doughnuts. "Help yourselves, guys," Sam said, setting the box on the table. "We've got news."

As Wyatt and Kevin dove in, Sam gave a rundown of their meeting with Bruce Benedict. Garvin's plans to change his will. His research into the River Road property. And the other interested party—who might or might not be Marnie Wilson.

"So Garvin was digging into the land's history?" Wyatt asked, wiping a trace of glaze from his fingers.

Jo nodded. "Benedict didn't have details, but whatever Garvin found, it sounded like he was meeting someone about it."

"A few of his neighbors weren't home when I went up there yesterday. I'll revisit them." Kevin leaned back in his chair, tapping his pen on the desk. "But we still don't know if that other buyer is Marnie?"

"Not officially," Sam said. "But her interest lines up a little too well, especially with Convale throwing money her way."

A weight settled over the room. Lucy padded over to Jo, resting her head on Jo's knee. Jo scratched behind the dog's ears, appreciating the comfort.

The quiet shattered when Reese burst in, her face flushed with something close to alarm.

"What is it?" Sam asked, standing up.

Reese took a deep breath. "We got a hit on the DNA from the hair tie we found at Garvin's."

A spark of hope flashed in Jo's eyes. "Someone we know?"

Reese hesitated, glancing between Jo and Sam. "It wasn't a match in CODIS. But..." She paused, the words catching. "It matched someone in law enforcement."

Silence fell. Sam's voice was measured, careful. "Who, Reese?"

Reese swallowed. "It matched Jo."

The room went still. Jo felt like the floor had dropped beneath her. Lucy pressed closer, her warm weight the only thing steadying her in the shock.

Sam was the first to break the silence, his tone direct. "Jo, you were over there often, bringing him meals. Could you have left it behind?"

Jo shook her head firmly. "No way. I never took my hair out of the holder there."

Wyatt cleared his throat. "Maybe you took it down for a minute, adjusted it?"

"No," Jo said, her tone steady. "I'm sure of it."

"Maybe one fell out of your pocket?" Wyatt suggested.

Jo considered it but shook her head. "Unlikely. I don't carry extras on me."

An uneasy silence fell. Jo could feel her team-mates' eyes on her, their minds working through the implications. The unspoken question was clear: if she hadn't left the hair tie, then who had?

Sam ran a hand through his hair, his frustration barely contained. "Look, we all know Jo wouldn't hurt Garvin. But we also can't ignore this. We have to do this by the book, Jo. No shortcuts."

Jo straightened, meeting his gaze head-on. "I wouldn't have it any other way."

Wyatt leaned forward, his eyes narrowed in thought. "When was the last time you saw him, Jo?"

Jo took a steadying breath, recalling. "Four days before he died. Brought him some of Bridget's soup. We talked on the porch, but I didn't go inside because he was a little under the weather."

"And you're sure you didn't leave anything behind?" Sam pressed.

Jo looked him in the eye, her voice unwavering. "Positive. I checked in the mirror before leaving that day. My hair was tied back, and it stayed that way."

Kevin tapped his pen on his desk, brow furrowed. "So if you didn't leave it... someone planted it."

The realization hit them all at once. Reese broke the silence, voicing the conclusion they'd all reached. "Someone's framing Jo."

CHAPTER THIRTEEN

Later that afternoon, Jo sat at her desk, her mind still reeling from the revelation that someone was trying to frame her. She'd gone through several emotions since finding out, but now, she was just plain mad.

Sam approached, his footsteps heavy with concern. He pulled up a chair, sitting down beside her. "How are you holding up?" he asked, his voice low and gentle.

Jo looked up. "Fine. Angry. More determined than ever to find who did this."

"Right. And why. I mean, is it something against you? What was the reason for leaving something that points to you. Or maybe they just happened to find the hair tie and used it to muddy the waters?"

Jo's hand instinctively went to her ponytail, which was tied with the very same ties. "I doubt it. It's not like I take it out much, and when I do, I put the tie around my wrist."

"Are you missing one?"

Jo shrugged. "Don't think so. Hard to tell, though. I buy them by the package and don't exactly keep an inventory or anything."

Wyatt and Kevin, who had been hovering nearby, exchanged glances before joining the conversation. Wyatt leaned against a nearby desk, his arms crossed. "We need to figure out where they could have gotten your hair from," he said, his tone analytical. "It might give us a lead on who's behind this."

Kevin nodded in agreement. "Any ideas, Jo? Have you noticed anything strange at your place lately? Any signs of a break-in?"

The thought sent a chill down Jo's spine. "God, I hope not," she said, her voice barely above a whisper. "The idea of someone being in my house, going through my things..." She shuddered, unable to finish the sentence.

Sam's jaw tightened, his protective instincts kicking in. "Let's not jump to conclusions. There might be a simpler explanation."

Wyatt nodded, his brow furrowed in thought.

"He's right. Think about it, Jo. Your hair is probably all over this station. Near your desk, in the cruiser…"

"Not to mention the countless places around town where you might have lost a few strands," Kevin added. "It wouldn't be hard for someone to collect a sample without breaking into your house."

Jo felt a small wave of relief wash over her. "That… That actually makes me feel a bit better," she admitted. "But that means they'd have to work hard and with intention to just find some hairs."

Sam placed a reassuring hand on her shoulder. "We'll figure this out, Jo. Whoever's behind this, we'll find them."

"I still have some of Garvin's neighbors to talk to who weren't home when I went there earlier. Hopefully, one of them saw something, and we'll get a lead," Kevin said.

Just as Jo was starting to feel a glimmer of hope, the squad room door swung open. Mayor Henley Jamison strode in, his face set in a grim expression. The room fell silent, tension crackling in the air as the mayor approached.

"Afternoon, everyone," Jamison said, his voice clipped and formal. His eyes landed on Jo, and she felt her stomach drop. "Sergeant Harris, I need to speak with you. Chief Mason, you should be present for this as well."

Sam stood, his posture stiff. "What's this about, Mayor?"

Jamison glanced around the room, noting the curious faces of Wyatt and Kevin. "Perhaps we should step into your office, Chief."

"Anything you have to say to me, you can say in front of my team," Jo said, rising to her feet. She squared her shoulders, meeting the mayor's gaze steadily.

Jamison hesitated for a moment then nodded. "Very well. Sergeant Harris, in light of recent developments, I'm afraid I have to relieve you of duty, effective immediately."

The words hit Jo like a physical blow. She heard Sam's sharp intake of breath beside her, felt the shock ripple through the room. "What?" she managed to say, her voice barely audible.

"Mayor, this is completely unnecessary," Sam began, his tone sharp with anger. "Jo is a victim here, not a suspect. We believe someone is trying to frame her."

Jamison held up a hand, cutting off Sam's protest. "I understand your position, Chief. But the fact remains that evidence linking Sergeant Harris to the crime scene has been found. It would be highly improper for her to continue working on this case."

Jo felt as if the floor was tilting beneath her feet. She gripped the edge of her desk, steadying herself. "Mayor Jamison, I assure you, I had nothing to do with Garvin's death. I would never—"

"I'm not accusing you of anything, Sergeant," Jamison interrupted, his tone softening slightly. "But we have to consider the optics of the situation. If word gets out that you're still on the case despite this evidence, it could compromise the entire investigation. Not to mention..." He trailed off, looking uncomfortable.

"Not to mention what?" Sam pressed, his voice tight with barely contained anger.

Jamison sighed. "Not to mention the potential impact on my reelection campaign. Marnie Wilson would seize on this in a heartbeat, using it to paint my administration as corrupt or incompetent."

Jo felt a surge of bitter disappointment. Of course, it all came down to politics. She opened her mouth to argue, but to her surprise, Sam beat her to it.

"With all due respect, Mayor," Sam said, his voice low and dangerous, "if you think I'm going to let you sacrifice one of my best officers for the sake of your campaign—"

"Sam," Jo interrupted, placing a hand on his arm. She could feel the tension thrumming through him, knew he was on the verge of saying something he couldn't take back. "It's okay."

Sam turned to her, disbelief etched on his face. "Jo, you can't be serious. This isn't right."

Jo met his gaze, trying to convey her resolve. "Maybe not, but the mayor has a point. We can't risk compromising the investigation." She turned back to Jamison, her voice steady despite the turmoil inside her. "I understand, Mayor. I'll step down for now."

Jamison nodded, looking relieved. "Thank you for your understanding, Sergeant. I assure you, this is temporary. Once this matter is cleared up—"

"Save it," Sam growled, still glaring at the mayor.

Jo moved to her desk, pulling out her badge and gun. She held them for a moment, feeling their familiar weight in her hands. Then, with a deep breath, she held them out to Sam. "I guess you should take these," she said softly.

Sam stared at the offered items, his face a mask of conflicting emotions. For a moment, Jo thought he might refuse. Then, with a barely perceptible nod, he took them from her, his fingers brushing hers in a gesture of silent support.

As the tense scene unfolded, movement from the

top of the filing cabinet caught Jo's eye. Major had been observing the proceedings with his usual air of feline indifference. Now, as Jamison stood near the cabinet, Major leaned forward, snaking his paw out slowly. With one quick swipe, he jabbed Henley in the shoulder.

"Ouch!" Henley whirled around. The cat simply sat there, looking all innocent. "Did you just scratch me?" Henley brushed at his shoulder.

"I didn't see anything, did you?" Kevin looked at Wyatt and Sam, who all shook their heads.

"I'll clear out my desk," Jo said.

"There's no need for that," Jamison said quickly. "As I said, this is temporary. Just... take some time off. We'll sort this out."

Jo nodded.

Jamison looked relieved to end the uncomfortable scene. "I'm sure Chief Mason will keep you informed of any developments."

CHAPTER FOURTEEN

Jo may have been relieved of duty, but that didn't mean she'd sit around while someone framed her for murder. She drove home fast, her mind set on how to fight back.

When she parked, she noticed Pickles under the porch rocking chair, tail flicking. "Hey, Pickles," she said, scratching the cat's head. "At least you're not out to get me."

Inside, she tossed her keys on the counter, grabbed a can of cat food, and spooned it into a dish. "Here you go, buddy." She glanced at Finn, her goldfish, circling his bowl, oblivious. "Must be nice, Finn. No setups in your world."

Jo set the dish on the porch for Pickles, watching as he approached. "Listen, buddy," she murmured, settling into the rocker. "I don't know how much longer we'll be here. So think about coming inside so I can take you to the next place." She ran a hand over her face, frustration simmering. "One step at a time, right?"

She stood, feeling the weight of the investigation. Inside her bedroom, the old armoire stood like a fortress, holding a mix of memories and the skeletons she'd rather leave untouched. But she needed space for a new investigation board, one focused on clearing her name. She opened the armoire, her gaze brushing over a box marked with her youngest sister's name.

"Tammy." Her chest tightened, but she shook it off. "Not now," she whispered, pushing the box aside.

Instead, she started tacking notes and timelines to the inside of the doors. What had Garvin found, and who wanted her out of the way?

An hour later, Jo stepped back, staring at the bare beginnings of her board. She needed an outsider's perspective—someone who could dig around, no questions asked. She pulled out her phone, scrolling to Mick's number.

It rang twice before she heard his familiar, gruff voice. "Gervasi."

"Mick, it's Jo. I need a hand."

A pause. "I heard what happened. You holding up?"

"Not going down without a fight," she replied. "Can you come over?"

"Twenty minutes." Mick hung up, no more questions asked.

While she waited, Jo paced the living room, mind racing. Who had the access to frame her? Who'd gain from Garvin's death? She had to break this open, fast.

Twenty minutes later, the rumble of Mick's truck pulled her from her thoughts. She opened the door as he climbed out, his gaze scanning her yard with a practiced eye.

"Thanks for coming," she said.

He nodded. "You know I've got your back." His gaze was sharp, searching, as he stepped inside.

Jo led him to the bedroom, motioning to her makeshift investigation board. "It's not much," she said, but he was already studying it.

Mick crossed his arms, his brow furrowed. "All right. Walk me through it."

For the next hour, she recounted everything—the body, the hair tie, the DNA match. Mick listened without interrupting, occasionally jotting a quick note.

"So, whoever it is got ahold of your hair. That's

personal." Mick leaned against the wall, eyes narrowing. "Any ideas?"

Jo shook her head, frustration biting into her words. "None. Sure, I've crossed a few people, but this feels different. This feels... close."

"What about Marnie Wilson?" Mick asked. "She's got eyes on Garvin's land, right? And a detective on the hook for murder would make her campaign look a lot cleaner."

Jo frowned. "Maybe. But there's got to be more to it. It doesn't add up."

"Or his kids," Mick added. "They'd lose a payout if Garvin went through with that will change."

Jo considered it, frustration sparking. "But I don't know them, and they don't know me. How would they get ahold of my hair?"

"Maybe they didn't," Mick said. "Could be someone working with them. Someone with access to you." He shook his head. "We'll get to the bottom of it."

Jo felt a surge of gratitude, the weight in her chest easing for the first time all day. "Thanks, Mick. I don't know what I'd do without you."

He waved it off. "What are friends for?"

CHAPTER FIFTEEN

Kevin pulled up to the bakery, his heart rate picking up slightly as he caught sight of Bridget through the window. He took a deep breath, reminding himself that he was only here for cookies. At least, that was what he'd tell her. The truth was, he couldn't stop thinking about Bridget, and any excuse to see her was good enough for him.

As he pushed open the door, the bell chimed softly. Bridget looked up, a smile spreading across her face when she saw him. Kevin felt a warmth in his chest at her reaction.

"Hey, stranger," Bridget called out. "What brings you by?"

Kevin shrugged, trying to appear casual. "Oh, you know, just had a craving for some of your famous chocolate chip cookies." He approached the counter, his eyes scanning the empty bakery. "Slow day?"

Bridget nodded, brushing a stray lock of hair behind her ear. "Yeah, it's been pretty quiet. But that means I get to experiment with some new recipes." She gestured to a tray of brownies cooling on the rack behind her. "I'm putting together a care package for Jo. Reese told me what happened."

Kevin's mood sobered at the mention of Jo. "Yeah, it's a mess. The mayor relieving her of duty... It's ridiculous."

"I can't believe anyone would think Jo had anything to do with Garvin's murder," Bridget said, her voice laced with concern.

Kevin leaned against the counter, lowering his voice even though they were alone. "Of course, we don't think for a minute she had anything to do with it. We'll investigate officially, and then unofficially, we'll help with whatever she needs."

Bridget smiled, a mischievous glint in her eye. "If I know Jo, she's probably already out there tailing suspects."

Kevin chuckled, picturing Jo staking out potential leads from her car. "You're probably right. She's not one to sit idle, especially when her reputation is on the line and I just got a lead that might help her."

Bridget raised a brow, and he continued, "I just got back from talking to a neighbor. A red Prius was seen near Garvin's property around the time of the murder. The neighbor thinks they remember a few numbers on the plate."

Bridget's brow furrowed. "A few numbers? Can you really figure out who it is from that?"

"Maybe," Kevin replied. "Reese is running it through the database along with the car description. We're hoping for a match."

"Let's hope," Bridget said.

As Bridget continued to pack the brownies, Kevin found himself watching her hands move deftly, wrapping each treat with care. He couldn't help but admire her dedication to her sister, her kindness evident in every gesture.

"You know," Kevin started, his voice hesitant, "I've been thinking. Could this be related to your situation?"

Bridget paused, her eyes meeting his. "I don't think so. This feels different. But I appreciate you thinking about it."

Kevin nodded, but he couldn't shake the nagging feeling that everything was connected somehow. He must have let his worry show on his face because Bridget stopped what she was doing and gave him a searching look.

"Kevin, what's going on? You're acting weird."

He hesitated, torn between his desire to protect Bridget and his need for her help. Finally, he sighed. "I got a note on my car. It was a warning telling me to be careful what I dig for. I think it has to do with the thumb drive. Someone's watching us, Bridget. Maybe we shouldn't be seen together so much."

Bridget's eyes widened then narrowed with determination. "What? No way. Don't forget; you saved my sister. I'm in this thing. Don't shut me out now!"

Her fierce loyalty both touched and worried Kevin. He didn't want to put her in danger, but he also knew he couldn't solve this alone. "All right, all right," he conceded. "But we need to be careful."

"So, what's our next move?" Bridget asked, leaning in closer.

"Listen," Kevin said, glancing at his watch, "we probably shouldn't talk about this here. You still coming over tomorrow night?"

Bridget nodded. "Yep, and I have a turkey meatloaf recipe I've been dying to try. I'll bring that over for dinner."

Kevin felt a flutter in his stomach at the thought of sharing a meal with Bridget. "That sounds perfect," he said, trying to keep his voice steady.

As he prepared to leave, Kevin found himself

lingering, reluctant to end their conversation. He watched as Bridget finished packing the care package for Jo, admiring her thoughtfulness.

"You're a good sister, you know that?" he said softly.

Bridget looked up, a hint of vulnerability in her eyes. "I'm trying to be. After everything Jo's done for me... I just want to be there for her now."

Kevin nodded, understanding all too well the weight of past mistakes and the desire to make things right. "Well, I think you're doing a great job."

As he finally turned to leave, Kevin's mind was racing. He was excited about the prospect of spending more time with Bridget, but he couldn't shake the feeling that they were getting into something bigger than they realized.

Walking to his car, Kevin made a mental note to double-check his home security system before Bridget came over. He couldn't risk anything happening to her. As he drove away, he caught sight of Bridget in his rearview mirror, still visible through the bakery window. She was smiling, and that made Kevin smile too.

CHAPTER SIXTEEN

W yatt shifted uncomfortably in his seat, his eyes fixed on Marnie's campaign headquarters across the street. The clock on his dashboard read 9:47 p.m., and he'd been parked in the same spot for over an hour. He drummed his fingers on the steering wheel, his other hand absently tracing the outline of the tattoo hidden beneath his sleeve.

The tattoo was a constant reminder of the secret he carried, a burden that weighed heavily on his conscience. Wyatt often wondered if his colleagues suspected anything. He knew Kevin had skeletons in the closet, but Wyatt doubted they were as dark as his own.

A movement caught his eye, pulling him from his

thoughts. Marnie Wilson emerged from the building, her honey-blond hair gleaming under the streetlights. Wyatt straightened in his seat, adrenaline coursing through his veins as he watched her climb into her car.

As Marnie pulled away from the curb, Wyatt counted to ten before starting his engine. He eased into traffic, maintaining a careful distance as he followed her through the quiet streets of White Rock.

The chase gave Wyatt a rush, reminding him of his younger days when he'd first discovered his talent for computers. Back then, it had been about the thrill of pushing boundaries, seeing how far he could go without getting caught. Now, those same skills were put to use for a greater purpose, even if the methods weren't always strictly by the book.

Marnie's car turned onto a familiar street, and Wyatt's eyebrows rose as he recognized her destination. The Thorne residence loomed ahead, its imposing facade a stark contrast to the more modest homes surrounding it.

Wyatt pulled over, killing his headlights as he watched Marnie park in the driveway. She exited her car and strode purposefully to the front door, which opened before she could even knock. Beryl Thorne's petite figure was silhouetted in the doorway for a moment before both women disappeared inside.

As he waited, Wyatt's mind wandered to the case at hand. Jo's suspension had hit the team hard, and he couldn't shake the feeling that Marnie was somehow involved. But how? And what was her connection to Beryl Thorne?

A few minutes later, the front door opened again. Marnie emerged, clutching a thick manila envelope to her chest. She hurried to her car, glancing around furtively before getting in and driving away.

Wyatt waited a beat before following, his curiosity piqued by the mysterious envelope. What could be so important that Marnie would make a late-night visit to Beryl Thorne to obtain it?

They drove for about fifteen minutes, leaving the residential area and entering a more industrial part of town. Marnie finally pulled up in front of a nondescript building with a small, unassuming sign that read Parker Studies.

Wyatt parked a block away, watching as Marnie entered the building with the envelope. He glanced at his watch—10:32 p.m. An odd time for a meeting, especially for someone running for mayor.

With Marnie out of sight, Wyatt pulled out his laptop. If there was one thing he excelled at, it was digging up information that others wanted to keep hidden. His fingers flew across the keyboard as he began his search on Parker Studies.

To his surprise and frustration, he found... nothing. No website, no business listings, not even a mention on social media. It was as if Parker Studies didn't exist at all.

Wyatt's brow furrowed as he dug deeper, employing some of his more questionable skills to breach firewalls and access restricted databases. Still, he came up empty-handed. Whoever was behind Parker Studies had gone to great lengths to keep their operation off the grid.

Two hours crawled by, each minute feeling like an eternity as Wyatt alternated between watching the building and attempting to uncover any information about Parker Studies. His eyes were starting to burn from staring at the computer screen when movement at the building's entrance caught his attention.

Marnie emerged, her face partially obscured by the shadows. Wyatt noticed immediately that she no longer carried the manila envelope. Whatever had been inside, she'd left it at Parker Studies.

As Marnie's car pulled away from the curb, Wyatt discreetly followed at a safe distance. He followed her to her home, noting the moment when the lights in her house flickered off one by one. Sighing, he decided it was time to call it a night.

On the drive back to his own place, Wyatt's mind buzzed with new questions. What exactly were the Parker Studies, and how did they connect to Marnie Wilson? And did this have anything to do with Garvin McDaniels's murder?

CHAPTER SEVENTEEN

The next morning, Sam arrived at the station early, his mind still churning over Jo's suspension. In the reception area, Reese was hunched over her computer, her brow furrowed in concentration.

"Morning, Reese," Sam called out. "You're here early."

Reese looked up, her eyes bright with excitement. "Chief! I've got something. The program spit out a match for that partial plate and car description that Kevin got from the neighbor."

Sam's pulse quickened as he moved to stand behind Reese's chair. "What have you got?"

"It's registered to a Clara Hartwell," Reese reported, pulling up the information on her screen. "She's a local land surveyor and historical researcher."

Sam leaned in, studying the details. "Good work, Reese. Any priors?"

Reese shook her head. "Nothing. Clean record. She's been a resident of White Rock for over twenty years."

Sam straightened, his mind already formulating a plan. "All right, I'm going to pay Ms. Hartwell a visit. Can you send her address to my phone?"

"Already done, Chief," Reese replied with a smile.

Sam turned to Lucy, who was sitting quietly, watching their conversation as if she could understand them. "Looks like we're heading back out."

Once in the car, Sam pulled out his phone and dialed Jo's number.

She answered on the second ring. "Harris."

"Jo, it's Sam. We've got a lead on a car that was seen near Garvin's property the day he died."

He could hear the rustling of papers in the background as Jo spoke. "That's great news. What have you got?"

Sam filled her in on Clara Hartwell as he navigated the streets of White Rock. "Does the name ring any bells?"

There was a pause on the other end of the line. "No, I don't know her. Why would she be trying to frame me?"

"That's what we're going to find out," Sam replied, his voice grim. "I'm heading over to interview her now. I'll keep you posted."

"Thanks, Sam," Jo said, her voice softening. "Be careful, okay?"

"Always am," Sam assured her before ending the call.

As they pulled up to Clara Hartwell's modest Cape Cod, Sam noted the red Prius in the driveway. The gardens were tidy, neat as a pin, like Clara's reputation. He climbed out, Lucy padding beside him, tail wagging.

A woman answered the door, looking from Sam to Lucy with mild curiosity.

"Ms. Hartwell?" Sam held up his badge. "Chief Sam Mason. I was hoping to ask you a few questions."

Clara Hartwell's brows lifted. "Chief Mason," she said, her tone polite but guarded. "Of course. Come in."

She led him into a cozy, book-lined living room. History texts and old maps covered the walls. Clara gestured to a chair as she took her own seat, eyeing Lucy.

"This is our police K-9, Lucy," Sam said.

Clara smiled down at Lucy as the dog sat on the floor beside Sam's chair.

"All right, then," Clara said, settling in. "How can I help you?"

"Were you at Garvin McDaniels's place two days ago?"

She nodded, a slight frown creasing her brow. "Yes, I was very sorry to hear about his passing. I had an appointment with him that afternoon, in fact. He'd asked me to look into some old land records for a property on River Road."

"Any idea why he suddenly got interested in the property?" Sam asked.

Clara's gaze drifted as she thought it over. "He said it was land he'd inherited years ago but never paid much attention to. Then, recently, he got the impression it could be valuable." She glanced back at Sam. "He didn't say why. Just wanted to know if there was anything of historical interest."

"Did you find anything?" Sam prompted.

She rose, moving to a nearby bookshelf and pulling out a large folder. "Some old surveys show unusual features on the land. Nothing confirmed, but he was intrigued." She opened the folder, revealing faded blueprints and yellowed documents. "I gave Garvin copies of these."

Sam looked over the maps and documents, his mind racing. He hadn't seen anything like this in

Garvin's house. "Any chance you remember where he put them?"

"He took them back to his place, said he'd look them over. But..." She paused. "You think they're missing?"

"It's possible." Sam tucked away that thought for later. "Did you notice anything unusual around the property? Strange activity?"

Clara thought for a moment then shook her head. "Nope, just the normal property map. Garvin was fine when I left."

"What time was that?"

"Four o'clock."

Sam nodded, making a mental note. "Thank you, Ms. Hartwell. This has been helpful."

She walked him to the door, giving Lucy a quick scratch behind the ears. "Let me know if you need anything else, Chief."

Back in the car, Sam's mind raced. If those blue-prints and documents were missing, it could mean they held the key to the motive behind Garvin's death. He'd have to recheck the house, this time with a sharper eye.

CHAPTER EIGHTEEN

S am filled his coffee mug and turned to face the squad room. The absence of Jo felt like a missing limb. Lucy must have felt it too. She padded over to Jo's empty desk and sniffed at her chair, letting out a soft whine.

"I know, girl," Sam said softly, his voice tinged with a mixture of frustration and determination. "We'll get her back soon."

As if on cue, Major sauntered across the room and leapt onto Jo's desk. The black cat circled once before settling into a patch of sunlight, his green eyes surveying the room with regal indifference.

"All right, team," Sam began, his voice cutting through the heavy silence. "We've got a lot to cover, and time isn't on our side. Let's start with what we know."

Reese spoke up first. "Chief, I've been digging into Clara Hartwell's background. She checks out clean and was at work at the time Garvin died."

Sam nodded, processing the information. "Good work, Reese. So she's not the killer, but is the information she was looking into the reason he was killed?"

Kevin leaned forward, his brow furrowed. "Why would that get him killed? It doesn't make sense."

"Maybe it does," Wyatt interjected, his fingers tapping rapidly on his laptop keyboard. "If the land has historical value, it could interfere with someone's plans to exploit it somehow."

Sam's eyes narrowed. "Maybe. We're missing something crucial here." He turned to face the team fully. "When I spoke with Clara, she mentioned leaving blueprints and historical documents with Garvin. But we didn't find any of that during our initial search of his house."

Wyatt tapped his pencil on the desk. "We weren't necessarily looking. We were focused on clues to the killer."

Reese's eyes widened. "You think the killer took them?"

"It's possible," Sam replied. "Or Garvin hid them

somewhere we didn't think to look. Either way, we need to go back and search his place again, this time with a focus on finding those documents. Has that bronze statue Jo mentioned turned up anywhere?"

Reese shook her head. "I've been searching eBay and Marketplace, called antique dealers and auctioneers, but have nothing."

"John Dudley says the way the wounds were on the body indicate Garvin could have been killed by something like that, but he'd need the actual statue to say for sure," Kevin said.

"I found something interesting about Marnie Wilson," Wyatt said. "I tailed her last night, and things got weird fast."

Kevin raised an eyebrow. "Weird how?"

"She made a late-night visit to Beryl Thorne's place," Wyatt explained, his words coming out in a rush. "Left with a manila envelope then drove to some place called Parker Studies. Stayed there for a couple of hours, left without the envelope."

Sam's brow furrowed. "Parker Studies? Never heard of it."

"That's because it doesn't exist," Wyatt said, his voice tinged with frustration. "At least, not officially. I couldn't find a single trace of it online or in any business registries."

Reese leaned in, her curiosity piqued. "A front for something illegal?"

Sam nodded slowly, his mind racing. "Could be. But what's the connection to Garvin's murder and Jo's frame-up?"

Kevin stood up, pacing the room as he thought out loud. "Okay, let's break this down. We've got Garvin, who's considering selling his land. Then he finds out it might have historical significance and gets cold feet. Next thing we know, he's dead, and Jo's being framed for it."

"And now we've got Marnie Wilson, who's running for mayor, making secret late-night visits to Beryl Thorne and this mysterious Parker Studies place," Wyatt added.

Sam's eyes narrowed as he pieced it together. "It all comes back to the land. Whatever's on that property, it's valuable enough to kill for."

"But how does Jo fit into all this?" Reese asked, her voice laced with concern.

Sam shook his head, frustration evident in his voice. "I don't know yet. But I'm willing to bet those missing blueprints and documents hold the answer."

As Sam spoke, Lucy suddenly perked up, her ears twitching. She trotted over to a corner of the room where a stack of old case files had accumulated over the years. With determined focus, she began to dig, sending papers flying.

"Lucy, what are you doing?" Sam called out, moving toward the dog.

The German Shepherd pulled her head out of the pile, and to everyone's surprise, she had the station's infamous octopus toy clamped firmly in her jaws. It was the same toy that had been the source of an ongoing feud between Lucy and Major.

Kevin chuckled, shaking his head. "So that's where she hid it. Clever girl."

Major, who had been lounging on Jo's desk, sat up straight, his green eyes narrowing as he watched Lucy trot to the sunny corner of the room. The dog settled down, placing the toy protectively between her paws, looking quite pleased with herself.

Sam couldn't help but smile at the canine's antics but quickly refocused on the task at hand. "All right, Lucy, don't get too comfortable. We're heading back to Garvin McDaniels's place." He turned to Kevin. "You up for a second look?"

Kevin nodded, already reaching for his jacket. "Absolutely, Chief. Maybe we'll spot something we missed the first time around."

"Good," Sam replied then shifted his attention to Wyatt. "I need you to keep digging into this Parker

Studies angle. There's got to be something there. Check property records, shell companies, anything that might give us a lead."

Wyatt's fingers were already flying across his keyboard. "On it, Chief. I'll let you know the moment I find anything suspicious."

"Reese," Sam continued, "I want you to go through our records. See if there are any other cases involving land disputes or historical property claims in the area. Maybe we'll find a pattern."

"You got it," Reese replied, her voice filled with determination.

As Sam and Kevin prepared to leave, Lucy reluctantly got up, still clutching her prized toy. Major watched from his perch, tail twitching in annoyance.

"Sorry, Major," Sam said to the cat. "Looks like Lucy won this round."

CHAPTER NINETEEN

Sam pulled up to Garvin McDaniels's house and glanced at Kevin in the passenger seat, noting the determined set of his jaw. "Ready for round two?" Sam asked, killing the engine.

Kevin nodded, his eyes already scanning the property. "Let's hope we find something this time."

As they exited the car, Lucy bounded out, her nose immediately to the ground. Sam watched her, a small smile tugging at his lips. If anyone could find something they'd missed, it would be Lucy.

"All right, girl," Sam said, patting her head. "Show us what you've got."

They approached the house, their footsteps crunching on the icy remnants of snow. The crime scene tape fluttered in the breeze.

Sam took a deep breath as they entered, the familiar scent of the house hitting him. It was a mixture of old wood, dust, and the lingering metallic tang of blood. He pushed aside the twinge of discomfort, focusing on the task at hand.

"Let's start in the study," Sam suggested, leading the way down the narrow hallway.

The study was small, dominated by a large oak desk and floor-to-ceiling bookshelves. Lucy immediately began sniffing around the baseboards while Kevin moved to the desk.

"If I were hiding important documents," Kevin mused, running his hands along the underside of the desk, "where would I put them?"

Sam started examining the bookshelves, pulling out volumes at random and flipping through them. "Maybe between the pages of a book? Or behind them?"

After thoroughly combing through the study and coming up empty-handed, they moved on to the bedroom. It was sparsely furnished, with just a bed, a nightstand, and an old wardrobe.

Lucy jumped onto the bed, her nose working overtime as she sniffed the pillows and blankets. Sam couldn't help but chuckle at her enthusiasm.

"Easy, girl," he said, gently pulling her off the bed. "Let's try not to disturb things too much."

Kevin was already rifling through the wardrobe, pushing aside old coats and sweaters. "Nothing here but mothballs," he said, wrinkling his nose at the musty smell.

Sam knelt down, peering under the bed. "Nothing here either," he sighed, standing up and brushing dust from his knees.

They continued through the house, methodically searching each room. The kitchen yielded nothing but expired cans of soup and a drawerful of takeout menus. The bathroom was equally unproductive, though Lucy seemed particularly interested in sniffing around the toilet.

"Come on, Lucy," Sam called, gently tugging her leash. "I don't think Garvin hid any maps in there."

As they made their way back to the living room, Sam felt a growing sense of frustration. They'd been so sure they would find something, but the house seemed determined to keep its secrets.

"Maybe the killer did take those maps," Kevin suggested, running a hand through his hair.

Sam nodded, considering the possibility. "You might be right. If someone took them after killing Garvin, we're not going to find them here."

"And that gives us motive."

Lucy, seemingly sensing their disappointment, let out a soft whine. Sam reached down to scratch behind her ears, grateful for her unwavering support.

"It's okay, girl," he murmured. "You did your best."

As they prepared to leave, Sam took one last look around the living room. The crime scene markings were still visible, stark reminders of the violence that had occurred here. He shook his head, trying to clear the image of Garvin's body from his mind.

"Let's head out," he said to Kevin.

They stepped out onto the front porch, the cool air a welcome relief after the stuffiness of the house. Sam was about to descend the steps when Lucy suddenly stiffened, her ears perking up.

Before either man could react, Lucy darted forward, barking excitedly. She began pawing at a patch of melting snow near the base of the porch steps.

"Lucy, what is it?" Sam called, hurrying down to join her.

Beneath the layer of fluffy snow that had fallen after Garvin's death was another layer of icy snow, and in that icy snow was a footprint. The killer's? It was only a partial, and there was something else. The snow was tinged blue. Sam's heart rate quickened as he knelt down for a closer look.

"Kevin, get a photo of this, and grab an evidence bag," he called over his shoulder, carefully brushing away more snow.

Kevin was by his side in an instant, evidence bag at the ready. Kevin took a few pictures of the partial shoe print, and then Sam gently scooped up a small amount of the blue-tinged snow, making sure to get some of the surrounding area as well.

"What do you think it is?" Kevin asked, peering at the bag as Sam sealed it.

Sam shook his head, his mind racing with possibilities. "I'm not sure. Dye from what the person was wearing? Might not be the killer's, but if Lucy thinks it's important, we'd better take it seriously."

"You mean like when you don't sort your laundry and the dye from the darks runs all over your white T-shirts," Kevin said.

Sam chuckled. "Exactly. Maybe the killer had new shoes."

As they walked back to the car, Sam's mind was buzzing with questions. What was that blue substance? How did it relate to Garvin's murder? And most importantly, could it help clear Jo's name?

He glanced at Lucy, who was trotting alongside him with her tail held high, looking immensely pleased with herself. Despite the lack of maps, Sam couldn't help but feel a renewed sense of hope. They might not have found what they came for, but thanks to Lucy, they'd found something potentially even more valuable.

"Let's get this back to the lab," Sam said as they climbed into the car. "And Kevin? Make sure Lucy gets an extra treat when we get back to the station. She's earned it."

Kevin grinned, reaching back to ruffle Lucy's fur. "You got it, Chief. One extra-large treat coming right up for our star detective."

CHAPTER TWENTY

Sam strode into the station, Lucy at his heels, with Kevin following close behind. The disappointment of not finding the maps at Garvin's house still weighed heavily on his mind, but the discovery of the mysterious blue substance gave him a glimmer of hope.

Wyatt looked up from his computer as they entered, his eyebrows raised in expectation. "Any luck at Garvin's place?"

Sam shook his head, sighing as he sank into his chair. "No maps, but Lucy found something interesting in the snow outside. We bagged it for the lab."

Kevin nodded, holding up the evidence bag. "It's some kind of blue substance. We're hoping it might give us a new lead."

Wyatt leaned back in his chair, his fingers

steepled in front of him. "Well, I wish I had better news on my end, but this Parker Studies place is a ghost. It's like they've gone out of their way to hide what they do."

Sam frowned, his mind turning over the implications. "That's not a good sign. If they're that determined to stay off the radar, they must be involved in something shady."

"And with Marnie Wilson making secret visits there..." Kevin trailed off, the unspoken conclusion hanging in the air.

Sam stood up, pacing the room as he thought out loud. "It doesn't look good for her, that's for sure. But what could she be involved in? And how does it tie into Garvin's murder?"

Wyatt shrugged, his expression grim. "I don't know, Chief, but if she becomes the next mayor, it could be a real problem for the town."

"All the more reason to figure out what she's up to," Sam said, his jaw set with determination. "I might have to pay a visit to Parker Studies myself, see what I can dig up."

Lucy, who had been curled up under Sam's desk, suddenly perked up, her ears twitching. Sam glanced down at her, a small smile tugging at his lips. "What do you think, girl? Ready for another adventure?"

Lucy's tail thumped against the floor in response, her eyes bright with eagerness.

Kevin chuckled, shaking his head. "I think that's a yes, Chief."

Sam nodded, his mind already planning his next move. "All right, let's see what the lab comes back with on that blue substance. In the meantime, Wyatt, keep digging into Parker Studies. There's got to be some way to find out more."

"On it, Chief," Wyatt replied, his fingers already flying across his keyboard.

Sam turned to Kevin. "And Kevin, I want you to take another look at the evidence from Garvin's house. Maybe there's something we overlooked, some clue that might tie into this Parker Studies angle."

Kevin nodded, his expression serious. "I'll go over everything with a fine-toothed comb, Chief."

With his team set to their tasks, Sam retreated to his office, Lucy following close behind. He closed the door, leaning against it for a moment as he collected his thoughts.

His eyes fell on the framed photo on his desk, a candid shot of him and Jo at last year's Fourth of July picnic. They were both laughing, their faces lit up with joy. The memory brought a bittersweet smile to his face.

"We're going to get you out of this, Jo," he murmured, his fingers brushing the frame. "I promise."

Lucy whined softly, as if sensing his mood. Sam reached down to scratch behind her ears, drawing comfort from her steady presence.

A sudden movement caught his eye, and he looked up to see Major sauntering into the office, his tail held high. The black cat leapt onto Sam's desk, green eyes blinking slowly as he surveyed the room.

"Hey, Major," Sam said, a wry smile tugging at his lips. "Come to offer your expertise?"

Major meowed in response then promptly curled up on top of Sam's paperwork, looking quite pleased with himself.

Sam shook his head, chuckling softly. "I'll take that as a yes."

With a sigh, he reached for his phone, scrolling through his contacts until he found Jo's number. He hesitated for a moment, his thumb hovering over the call button. What if she didn't want to hear from him? What if she blamed him for not finding the evidence to clear her name?

Pushing aside his doubts, Sam hit the call button, holding the phone to his ear as it rang.

"Sam?" Jo's voice was tinged with surprise as she answered. "What's going on?"

Sam took a deep breath, steeling himself. "We've got a new lead, Jo. Something called Parker Studies. Marnie Wilson's been making secret visits there, and Wyatt can't find any information on what they do."

There was a pause on the other end of the line, and Sam could almost hear the gears turning in Jo's head.

"Parker Studies?" she repeated, her tone thoughtful. "I've never heard of them. What do you think they're involved in?"

"I don't know," Sam admitted, frustration coloring his voice. "But whatever it is, it doesn't look good for Marnie."

Jo sighed, the sound heavy with weariness. "What about Clara Hartwell?"

Sam filled her in on how Garvin had been working with her on maps of the property and how they'd gone back to search Garvin's place for them.

"Did you find anything at Garvin's house?"

Sam hesitated, not wanting to disappoint her. "No, we didn't find the maps. But Lucy did find something interesting in the snow outside. We've sent it to the lab for analysis."

"Do you think Clara could be lying?" Jo asked, her voice sharp with suspicion. "Maybe she sent us on a wild-goose chase with those maps."

Sam shook his head even though Jo couldn't see

him. "No, I don't think so. She seemed genuinely concerned about the historical significance of Garvin's land. I think she's telling the truth."

Jo was quiet for a moment, and Sam could picture her pacing in her living room, her brow furrowed in thought.

"All right," she said finally, her voice filled with determination. "What's our next move?"

Sam glanced at his watch, an idea forming in his mind. "Let's meet at Holy Spirits after supper. We can bring Mick in, get everyone on the same page. Maybe he'll have some insight into this Parker Studies thing."

"Sounds good," Jo agreed, a hint of relief in her voice. "I'll see you there."

CHAPTER TWENTY-ONE

Jo pushed open the heavy doors of White Rock Town Hall, her footsteps echoing in the marble foyer. The building had the bones of a bygone era, with its high ceilings and polished floors. She found the office directory and quickly scanned it.

Town Land Surveyor - Room 14.

A few strides later, she knocked on the surveyor's door.

"Come in," called a woman's voice.

Inside, Jo found a cluttered office filled with old maps, blueprints, and stacks of files. A woman in her fifties looked up, her salt-and-pepper hair pulled into a no-nonsense bun.

"Clara Hartwell?" Jo asked, offering her hand. "Sergeant Harris, White Rock PD."

Clara nodded, shaking Jo's hand with a firm grip. "Chief Mason was at my house this morning. Told him everything I knew."

Jo hesitated for a moment,. She didn't feel good about omitting the fact that she was currently on leave, but she wanted to ask her own questions. She'd tell Sam tonight as she didn't want him to think she was going behind his back. Of course, Sam had done a great job, but Jo was looking at this from a little different perspective, and sometimes, it was better to ask the questions yourself.

"Thanks for that," Jo said, keeping her tone light. "I just had a few follow-ups. I understand Garvin McDaniels was interested in maps of his River Road property?"

Clara nodded slowly, sympathy flashing in her eyes. "Yes. Such a tragedy, what happened to him."

Jo kept her focus, pressing gently. "Did he say what he was looking for? Anything unusual?"

Clara's brows furrowed. "No. He was interested in the property lines but nothing specific. Just typical maps, as far as I knew. Same thing I told his son last week."

Jo blinked. "Garvin's son?"

Clara looked mildly surprised. "Yes, he stopped by last week too."

Jo felt a flicker of surprise. Sam hadn't mentioned the son. "So his son was here last week? You're sure about that?"

Clara looked momentarily unsure. "Well, yes. I remember because he asked about the property boundaries too."

Jo kept her tone steady. "Strange you didn't mention him to Chief Mason."

Clara's cheeks flushed slightly. "Maybe I was nervous. Or maybe I forgot." She frowned, as if annoyed with herself. "Chief Mason didn't ask if anyone else had been here."

Jo noted the slip-up, deciding to let it rest for now. "Did Garvin or his son look over anything specific? Mark anything?"

Clara shook her head, her gaze distant, as if trying to recall. "Not that I remember. Just property lines and abutters."

"Who are the abutters?"

Clara flipped open a file, glancing down. "Let's see... Horton family to the north; they've had that land forever. Whitfield estate to the east—been in probate for years. And to the south..." She looked up. "Convale Energy."

Jo's eyebrows shot up. "Convale?"

Clara nodded. "They own a significant chunk of land bordering Garvin's property."

Jo leaned back, taking that in. Convale Energy had been muscling in on White Rock for years, but she hadn't realized they were that close to Garvin's land.

"Interesting," Jo murmured. She watched Clara's reaction carefully. "Think they'd be interested in Garvin's property?"

Clara gave a small shrug. "Who knows with a company like that? They're always expanding."

Jo let the silence sit for a beat, her mind ticking through possibilities. Finally, she stood, nodding to Clara. "Thanks. You've been a big help."

Clara walked her to the door. "I hope you find what you're looking for, Sergeant."

Jo slipped out, her mind buzzing with new questions. So, Garvin's son had shown up at the surveyor's office—something Sam hadn't known. And Convale land abutted Garvin's, giving them a possible motive. She needed to share this with Sam—and soon. Luckily, she wouldn't have to wait long. It was almost time to meet at Holy Spirits.

CHAPTER TWENTY-TWO

Bridget set a steaming dish of turkey meatloaf on Kevin's kitchen table. "Dinner's ready," she announced.

"Smells incredible," Kevin said, pulling out a chair for her. "Seriously, you didn't have to do all this."

Bridget shrugged, brushing off the compliment. "You've been working hard, and I like cooking. Besides, you could use a good meal."

They ate in companionable silence until Bridget couldn't hold back her curiosity. "So," she asked casually, "any leads on the case?"

Kevin paused mid-bite, setting down his fork. "Nothing concrete, but we found the car I mentioned. Belongs to a land surveyor. Turns out Garvin was looking into the property where Jo's cottage is."

Bridget's brow furrowed. "Why would he be looking at that land?"

"Good question." Kevin took another bite, chewing thoughtfully. "Could be something about the land's history, maybe an ownership issue. We're still digging."

"Jo's been doing some digging of her own," Bridget said, smiling. "She even called Mick for backup."

Kevin chuckled. "I wouldn't be surprised if those two get to the bottom of it before we do."

Bridget smiled, pride flickering in her chest. Jo had always been the tough one, always looking out for everyone else. And even with her career on the line, here she was, still working to get to the truth.

"So," she ventured, "about that note. The one about the thumb drive. Any leads on who left it?"

Kevin's face darkened. He set down his fork, sighing. "No idea who left it or why."

Bridget reached across the table, resting a hand on his. "You'll figure it out."

Kevin nodded, his eyes lingering on hers for a beat. "I just can't shake the feeling that the thumb drive's bigger than we thought. What if the bodies at the Webster property had nothing to do with the thumb drive?"

"Or," Bridget said, leaning back, "what if we got the coordinates wrong?"

Kevin's eyes sparked. "Maybe. Or maybe they weren't coordinates at all. We just assumed because that's where we found the bodies."

They chewed over possibilities as they ate, lost in the thrill of the mystery until the plates were cleared. Bridget rinsed the dishes while Kevin dried them, the rhythm between them easy, like they'd been doing this for years.

Kevin broke the silence. "If those numbers aren't coordinates, they could be anything. A code, maybe?"

Bridget handed him a plate, considering. "Or dates? Maybe reference numbers?"

He nodded, intrigued. "All good options. What's our next move to figure it out?"

"Make a list of possibilities," Bridget suggested. "We check them off, see if they tie to that old narcotics case."

A grin broke across Kevin's face. "That's brilliant. Start with the most obvious, work our way down."

Bridget felt a surge of excitement. It felt good to be useful, to be part of something.

When the dishes were done, Kevin tossed the towel aside. "You know," he said, his voice quieter, "I appreciate the help. It's... nice having someone to work this through with."

Bridget's smile softened. "Glad to help. And it's good to feel... like I'm doing something real."

For a moment, it seemed like he might say more. But he cleared his throat, turning to grab a notebook from the counter. "So, let's get started on that list."

CHAPTER TWENTY-THREE

Jo spotted Sam and Mick as soon as she walked into Holy Spirits. They'd claimed their usual spots at the bar. Jo slid onto the stool beside Sam, who'd already ordered her a Coors Light. The place felt like a sanctuary, even with the low buzz of Friday night chatter around them.

"Hey, Harris," Mick greeted her, tipping his whiskey glass in her direction. "You're looking suspiciously well rested."

"Not having to work for an ogre does wonders," she shot back, giving Sam a grin. "But you look like you've seen better days."

Sam smirked, though his gaze held the weight of all they'd been dealing with. "Maybe I should try getting suspended. How's it working for you?"

"Only means I'm working for free now," she replied, taking a pull of her beer. "Met with Clara Hartwell today, the town surveyor. She mentioned something that could be a lead." She let the words hang, drawing both men's attention. "Garvin's son came by the surveyor's office last week asking about the River Road property too."

Sam's eyebrows shot up, and he set his glass down. "Did he now? Funny he didn't mention that to me. When I talked to Derek, he barely acted like he cared his father was looking into that land."

Jo's jaw tightened as she thought it over. "Seems like the son has a knack for leaving out details."

Sam took a slow sip of his drink. "Why would Derek go snooping around with a surveyor?"

Mick chimed in. "Kid's got money problems. I did some research. Got turned down for some loans."

Jo leaned in, lowering her voice. "The elk bronze. Garvin thought it was valuable—real valuable. Maybe Derek thought so too. If they argued, Derek could've tried to take it. If he needed money right away, he might not have wanted to wait for an inheritance."

Sam's gaze sharpened. "Or maybe he tried to hasten that along. But why look into the land?"

Jo thought back to her meeting with Clara. "Maybe he was trying to figure out the property's true value. If he thought Garvin was planning to sell, he'd want to know what it was worth. He wouldn't have known about the will change yet, so he was probably angling for inheritance. More property value, more to gain."

Mick gave a low whistle. "So, Garvin's looking into Convale, trying to figure out if he could get a better price on his land? His son starts sniffing around, trying to learn the same. It all sounds too close."

"More than close," Sam agreed.

Jo could feel the pieces shifting, each one clicking into place. "So Garvin's making inquiries—quietly, but he's doing his research. And if Convale caught wind of it? Could be they wanted him gone because they want that property."

Mick's mouth tightened as he set down his glass. "Or maybe they don't want someone to find out something about the property."

Jo's gaze drifted to the rows of bottles behind the bar, the colored light casting them in rich reds and blues. "But what? And if Derek is the killer, how did he get my hair to plant at the scene?"

The three of them sat in silence for a moment, the noise of the bar fading into the background. Jo took a long pull of her beer, letting the chill bite in her throat sharpen her focus.

"So," Mick said, swirling his whiskey thoughtfully, "what's the next move?"

Jo leaned back on her stool, crossing her arms. "We keep pulling the threads. Garvin's son was in town last week but didn't tell anyone, and now, his dad ends up dead. Seems like we need to talk to him."

Sam nodded. "Funeral's day after tomorrow. I'll leave him be until after that."

Mick raised his glass in a toast, his grin more sardonic than cheerful. "To the truth. May it dig itself up, sooner or later."

Jo clinked her bottle against his glass, feeling the steely edge of determination settle over her. "And to getting answers before any more bodies turn up. I'm getting back to my job even if it kills me."

CHAPTER TWENTY-FOUR

I t was already dark when Bridget pulled into the driveway of their little cottage. Jo's car wasn't there. She tugged her coat tighter against the chill as she approached the front steps. The porch light flickered above, casting a dim glow over the wooden boards, and Pickles, usually waiting at the door to greet her, was nowhere in sight.

A frown tugged at her lips. That was odd.

She was halfway to the door when she saw it. Her breath caught in her throat.

A single white sheet of paper, fluttering slightly in the breeze, was taped to the door. Large block letters scrawled in black marker. It was crude but unmistakable. A threat.

Secrets always come out.

Her heart pounded in her ears. It had to be for her. Someone knew. Someone had dug into her past—what she'd done. She stumbled forward, fingers trembling as she reached for the note, desperate to tear it down before Jo saw it. If Jo found out...

Just then, headlights illuminated her and froze her in place. Jo was pulling into the driveway. And she'd seen Bridget reaching for the note.

Bridget's fingers brushed the corner of the note, but it was too late. Jo was already out of the car and walking toward her, her gaze fixed on the note.

There was a beat of silence, and then Jo's body went rigid. Her eyes flicked from the note to the dark woods behind them, scanning the shadows with a tension that set Bridget's nerves on edge.

Jo's voice was low, dangerous. "This is about me."

Bridget's pulse quickened. No, no, it wasn't—Jo had it all wrong. But Jo's interpretation was immediate, her mind already racing. Her suspension, the frame job—of course, Jo would think the note was tied to that. Bridget felt a pang of guilt, a sick twist in her stomach that she couldn't confess her real fear, her real secret.

Jo's jaw tightened as she ripped the note off the door. "Whoever left this is trying to scare me off the case. They're desperate."

Bridget swallowed hard, trying to find her voice. "Jo... we don't know that. It could be—"

"Pickles," Jo interrupted, glancing around suddenly. "Where's Pickles?"

Bridget froze, her gaze darting around the porch. Now that Jo mentioned it, the cat still hadn't shown up. Someone had been here, and now, Pickles was gone. Anxiety gnawed at her insides.

"I... I don't know," she said, her voice barely above a whisper. "He's usually right here."

Jo's eyes darkened, and she pocketed the note. "Stay close."

Without waiting for a response, Jo stormed across the yard, scanning the area with sharp, deliberate movements. Bridget trailed behind her, her nerves fraying with each step. The trees loomed ominously around them, the wind picking up, rustling the branches like whispered threats.

Bridget's heart hammered in her chest, a mix of guilt and terror swirling inside her. Was this about Jo? About her suspension? Or was it for Bridget? The past she'd worked so hard to bury seemed to be clawing its way back to the surface, and the fear of it unraveling made her legs weak.

Jo crouched by the edge of the yard, her eyes scanning the ground. "No blood. No signs of struggle."

Bridget bit her lip, forcing herself to stay calm. But a gnawing panic kept rising inside her. Pickles wasn't merely a cat to her. He was a tether to something safe, something normal in a world that constantly threatened to rip her apart.

Jo stood, her face set in a hard line. "He could just be hiding... Or someone took him."

The words felt like a slap. Bridget stumbled forward, desperate to keep up with Jo's pace. "What... What do we do?"

Jo's eyes flicked toward the dark tree line again. "We'll find him. But first, we need to check inside. If they left the note, they might've been inside the house. Could be the person that tried to frame me."

Bridget swallowed hard, her throat tight. The thought of someone being inside their home made her skin crawl. She followed Jo back to the porch, her mind racing through every possible scenario. The note. Pickles. The things she hadn't told Jo. It was all colliding, and Bridget felt herself drowning in it.

Jo moved quickly, unlocking the front door and stepping inside with a controlled, quiet urgency. Bridget followed, her heart pounding louder with each step.

The house was dark and still, exactly as they'd left it. No signs of forced entry, no sign of anything out of place. But Bridget couldn't shake the feeling that something—someone—had been there. Watching. Waiting.

Jo's sharp gaze moved from room to room, and even without a word, Bridget could feel the rising tension in her sister's shoulders. It was the same tension she'd seen countless times before, the kind that came just before Jo made an arrest or kicked down a door. Jo was on edge, ready to spring into action.

Finally, Jo stopped in the middle of the living room, her eyes narrowing as she studied the note again.

"They're trying to scare me off," Jo said, more to herself than to Bridget. "But they're not going to get away with this."

Bridget stood frozen, her throat tight with unsaid words. Jo might be right. But if she wasn't, whoever left that note knew things that could ruin Bridget's new life.

CHAPTER TWENTY-FIVE

Jo didn't sleep very well that night and woke early. She wrapped her arms around herself as she stepped out onto the porch, her breath fogging in the crisp air. She glanced around, hoping—praying—for a glimpse of Pickles curled up on the porch, waiting for breakfast like he always did.

But the porch was empty. The box and blankets, usually occupied by the scruffy tabby, were empty.

She blew out a frustrated breath, her eyes darting over the yard. Pickles hadn't come back last night. She thought of the note still sitting ominously on the kitchen counter—*Secrets always come out*. It hadn't left her mind for a second. And now, with Pickles missing, she couldn't shake the feeling that the two things were connected.

Behind her, the door creaked as Bridget stepped outside, pulling her coat tight around her thin frame. Jo didn't have to ask to know that her sister had barely slept either.

"Still nothing?" Bridget asked, though the answer was obvious.

Jo shook her head. "No. And it's not like him to stay gone this long. He's been on the porch every night since it got cold."

Bridget rubbed her arms, her face pale in the cool morning light. "You think... You think the person who left the note did something to him?"

Jo's gut twisted at the question. It was the same fear that had gnawed at her all night. Whoever left that note—they weren't just trying to scare her. They wanted to send a message. And maybe Pickles had been part of that message.

"I don't know," Jo said finally, her voice low. "But we need to find him."

"I can't just sit here anymore," Bridget muttered, already stepping off the porch, her eyes scanning the edge of the woods. "I'm going to look for him. Now."

Jo nodded, slipping her phone out of her pocket and hitting Sam's contact. He'd said he would come by this morning to pick up the note as evidence. Maybe he could help them search. The phone rang twice before he picked up.

"I'm on my way," Sam said, his voice brisk but warm. "I'm about five minutes out. Just getting Lucy loaded into the truck."

Jo glanced back toward the woods, the trees casting long shadows over the yard. "Can you meet us in the woods behind the house? Pickles is still missing. I think... I think something's wrong."

There was a brief pause, then Sam's voice dropped, concerned. "I'll be there. Don't go too far in without me."

Jo hung up and turned to Bridget, who was already several steps ahead, pacing along the tree line.

"Sam's on his way," Jo called after her, jogging to catch up. "Let's start searching while we wait."

Bridget barely nodded, her eyes fixed on the trees, worry etched into her every movement. The two of them stepped into the woods, the morning light filtering weakly through the branches overhead. The air was damp, and the smell of wet earth clung to everything.

Jo's instincts kicked in as they began to search, her eyes sweeping the ground, looking for any sign of tracks, broken branches, something that might indicate someone had been there or where Pickles had gone. But there was nothing. No sign of him at all.

"Pickles!" Jo called out, her voice cutting through the silence.

Bridget echoed her call, but the woods remained still. Too still. Jo could feel the weight of the trees pressing in around them, the quiet making her skin prickle with unease.

Minutes stretched into what felt like hours as they moved deeper into the woods, their footsteps crunching on the underbrush. Jo's mind kept circling back to the note, to the possibility that someone had taken Pickles to send a message. Her frustration grew with each passing moment, the silence of the woods only feeding her anxiety.

Just as Jo was about to suggest they head back and wait for Sam, she heard it—a faint, almost imperceptible meow in the distance.

She froze, her heart skipping a beat. "Did you hear that?"

Bridget's head whipped around, her eyes wide. "Pickles?"

Jo strained to hear, her pulse quickening. There it was again, a soft, pathetic meow—fainter this time but unmistakable.

Jo started toward the sound, adrenaline spiking

through her as she and Bridget weaved through the trees, the meows growing louder, more desperate. But before they could get too far, the rumble of an engine caught Jo's ear. She glanced over her shoulder and saw the familiar White Rock Police Station Tahoe pulling into the driveway. Sam.

The moment Sam stepped out of the truck, Lucy leaped out behind him, her tail wagging but her ears pricked up, alert. Sam gave Jo a nod, and she waved him over, her heart pounding with the urgency of the situation.

"We heard him," Jo said as Sam jogged over. "He's close."

Sam glanced down at Lucy, who was already sniffing the air, her keen senses immediately kicking in. "Lucy can help. Let's follow her lead."

Without waiting for further instruction, Lucy's nose hit the ground, and she moved swiftly into the trees, her body low and her focus sharp. Jo felt a flicker of hope as they fell in behind her, Lucy guiding them deeper into the woods.

The meows were louder now, more frequent but still distant, as if they were coming from somewhere hidden. Jo's stomach twisted with the thought of what they might find—what could have happened to Pickles.

Lucy moved with purpose, weaving between trees

and over fallen branches, her nose pressed close to the ground. Her ears flicked with every sound, and Jo knew the dog was picking up something.

"Good girl, Lucy," Sam muttered as they followed her deeper into the woods. "Keep going."

Bridget's face was tense, her eyes darting from tree to tree as the meows grew louder, more insistent. Jo could feel the tightness in her chest as they pressed on, her mind racing with possibilities—none of them good.

Lucy suddenly stopped, her head jerking toward an old, rotted tree just ahead. Jo saw it before the others did—the mouth of a well, its crumbling stone rim barely visible beneath layers of overgrown moss and vines.

The meows echoed up from the darkness, faint but unmistakable.

"Oh no," Bridget whispered, her voice trembling. "He's down there."

Jo rushed forward, her flashlight beam sweeping over the well's edge as she knelt beside it. The dark hole yawned beneath her, and as she peered down, her breath caught in her throat.

There, huddled at the bottom, was Pickles—his fur matted, his eyes wide with terror. He let out another pathetic meow, his body trembling with fear.

"We need to get him out of there," Jo said, her voice tight with urgency.

Sam was already moving, pulling out his phone to call for backup. "Stay calm. We'll get him."

But even as the relief of finding Pickles washed over her, Jo couldn't shake the feeling that something darker was lurking just beneath the surface.

Had Pickles simply fallen into the well, or had someone thrown him in?

CHAPTER TWENTY-SIX

J o peered into the well at Pickles. The little cat looked terrified but seemed to be okay physically.

"Poor thing," Bridget whispered, her voice tight with worry. "How are we going to get him out of there?"

The well was deeper than Jo had expected, though thankfully, it was dry. The stone walls stretched down at least twenty feet, their surfaces slick with years of moss and decay. Pickles crouched on a small patch of earth at the bottom, his fur matted with dirt. He looked up at Jo, letting out another soft meow, as if begging her to come down to get him.

"We'll need a ladder," Sam said, his voice tense. He was already stepping back, scanning the area for anything that could help.

"There's one in my shed," Jo said, pulling herself away from the edge of the well.

They hurried back toward the house, veering toward the old shed near the edge of the property. The structure was weathered, its roof sagging from years of neglect, but it was still standing.

Sam pushed the door open with a creak, the hinges groaning in protest. Inside, the shed was filled with tools—rusted shovels, cracked flowerpots, and stacks of old wood. Jo's eyes scanned the cluttered space until they landed on an old ladder, leaning against the far wall.

"Perfect," Sam muttered, already grabbing it. He hefted the ladder over his shoulder with ease and turned back to Jo and Bridget. "This should do it."

They rushed back to the well, the cold biting at their skin. Jo's hands were shaking as she helped Sam set the ladder down into the well. It was almost too wide to fit, but thankfully, they managed to get it to the bottom.

Pickles hadn't moved from his spot at the bottom, his eyes still locked on them.

"I'll go," Sam said, his voice firm as he stepped over the rim of the well onto the first rung. He glanced at Jo, his expression unreadable. "You ready up here?"

Jo nodded, her breath puffing out in short, sharp clouds. "Yep."

Bridget hovered behind them, her hands clutched tightly together, eyes fixed on Pickles.

Sam began to climb down, his boots scraping against the slick stone walls. Jo gripped the top of the ladder, steadying it as he descended. The air inside the well was damp, musty, the smell of earth and moss rising up around them.

"Almost there," Sam called up, his voice echoing off the walls.

Jo leaned over the edge, watching as Sam reached the bottom. He crouched beside Pickles, speaking softly to the frightened cat. For a moment, Jo held her breath, praying that Pickles wouldn't dart away or make things harder. But the cat seemed too exhausted to put up a fight.

"It's okay, boy," Sam murmured, reaching out a hand. "Come here."

Pickles let out another pitiful meow, his body trembling as he took a tentative step toward Sam. Jo watched, her heart pounding, as Sam carefully lifted the cat into his arms. Relief washed over her. They had him.

But then, Sam froze.

Jo's grip on the ladder tightened as she watched

him go completely still. "Sam?" she called down, her voice edged with concern. "You okay?"

There was a beat of silence before Sam responded, his voice low, almost hesitant. "Yeah... but, uh, Pickles isn't the only thing down here."

Jo's heart lurched in her chest. She leaned farther over the edge, her knuckles white as she clung to the rim of the well. "What do you mean?"

Sam shifted, adjusting Pickles in one arm as he knelt down. "There's something else... under the dirt. I can see... bones."

Jo felt the blood drain from her face. "Bones?"

Sam's voice was steady but grim. "Yeah. Human."

"Are you sure?" Jo called down.

"Yeah, I'm sure," Sam said. He was crouched now, running his hand carefully over the ground. "Looks old. Part of the skull is exposed... and there's more buried beneath the dirt."

Jo swore under her breath, adrenaline spiking through her as she processed what this meant. A body in the well. How long had it been down there? And, more importantly, who was it?

She straightened, her mind already racing ahead. This was a crime scene now. They needed to call in forensics, secure the area. But first, they had to get Sam —and Pickles—out of the well.

"Okay, let's not touch anything else down there," Jo said, her voice steadying as she slipped back into professional mode. "Just bring Pickles up, and we'll deal with the rest."

"On it," Sam called back, his voice tight. He shifted again, making sure Pickles was secure in one arm as he began to climb back up the ladder. Jo watched him carefully, her hands still gripping the top of the ladder as he made his way up, slow and steady.

As Sam reached the top, Jo extended her arms, helping him lift Pickles over the edge and into Bridget's waiting hands. Bridget held the cat close to her chest, tears shining in her eyes as she whispered reassurances to him.

Jo barely had time to feel relieved before her attention snapped back to Sam, who was pulling himself out of the well. His jaw was tight as he straightened and dusted the dirt off his jacket.

"Definitely human," he muttered, wiping his hands on his jeans. "We're going to need a full team out here. Whoever that is down there... they've been dead a long time."

CHAPTER TWENTY-SEVEN

Wyatt's breath fogged the cold air as he snapped another picture of the bones lying at the bottom of the well. The flash bounced off the damp, moss-covered stone, throwing brief glimpses of the skeletal remains back up at him. A human skeleton, of all things, tangled in the mess of dirt and roots.

"This is going to be a real pain in the butt," John Dudley, the medical examiner, muttered as he surveyed the scene. "We'll need to haul it up piece by piece."

Wyatt grunted in agreement, but his attention wasn't fully on the logistics of retrieving the bones. His mind had been drifting ever since Sam mentioned the note earlier, when they were still back at the station.

Secrets always come out.

The words had sounded innocent enough when Sam first relayed them, but Wyatt had caught something—a flicker in Kevin's eyes, the way he glanced at Bridget as soon as Sam said the words. It wasn't long—just a moment—but Wyatt had been a cop long enough to know when people were hiding something.

He looked over at Kevin, who was standing a little apart from the group, hands jammed in his pockets, staring down at the well. Bridget was nearby, too, her arms wrapped around herself, her face pale as she watched the others work. They hadn't said much to each other, but there was something off in the way they were acting today. Something private.

Wyatt wasn't sure what to make of it, but the exchange between them had stuck with him. Was the note about Jo? Was Kevin involved in something he hadn't told anyone? What did Bridget have to do with it? He watched as Kevin walked over to help Sam with the ladder, his face tight with concentration, but Wyatt could see the tension in his movements. He was holding something back.

Wyatt shook the thoughts from his head, snapping another shot of the scene. Who was he to judge? He had his own secrets, things he hadn't shared with anyone. Secrets he wasn't sure he'd ever be able to talk about.

Subtly, Wyatt pulled his phone from his pocket and glanced down at the screen. He did it quickly, keeping the movement out of view of the others. No messages. Not from his mom, at least.

The last text she'd sent had been two days ago—a vague, guilt-laden message about needing money and how she "wasn't doing too good." He had ignored it. He didn't want to deal with her right now. Not after everything. But it had been eating at him ever since.

He couldn't ignore her forever.

Sam's voice pulled him back to the scene. "Wyatt, we need to rig the pulley. Let's get these bones up without damaging anything."

Wyatt moved to help Kevin, who was already securing the ladder into place, his movements quick and deliberate. Wyatt could feel the tension rolling off him—something more than the gruesome task of retrieving the bones.

"You all right?" Wyatt asked casually, his eyes on Kevin as they set up the pulley system.

Kevin gave a stiff nod, barely glancing at him. "Yeah. Just want to get this done."

Wyatt didn't push. He turned back to the well, watching as John Dudley directed the process. It was delicate work—noting the placement of everything before pulling the bones out carefully. Dudley was already snapping pictures from above, cataloging the position of each bone before they began the slow process of extraction.

"This skeleton's old," Dudley muttered as he knelt near the edge of the well. "Can't say how long it's been down there yet, but it's not recent. Not by a long shot."

Wyatt stepped back, watching as Kevin and Sam carefully hoisted the first set of bones out of the well. A femur, long and brittle, coated in dirt and rot. They moved slowly, methodically, passing the bones to Dudley, who placed them in an evidence bag with the kind of reverence usually reserved for the dead.

The process took time, each bone hauled up inch by inch, Wyatt's camera clicking every few minutes to capture the scene.

Finally, the last piece of the skeleton was pulled out—a cracked skull, yellowed and worn from years underground. The empty eye sockets stared up at Wyatt, hollow and silent, as if waiting for someone to ask the right questions.

Wyatt's grip tightened on his camera as he snapped another picture. This wasn't just a random body. This was connected to something bigger— Garvin, Convale, maybe even Marnie. And whatever it was, it was about to get a lot more complicated.

Dudley took a final set of pictures and stood,

wiping his hands on his pants. "We'll get this to the lab, run the tests. I'll let you know if I find anything."

Sam nodded, his eyes fixed on the skull. "Let's hope this gives us some answers."

Wyatt wasn't sure it would. Every new discovery seemed to raise more questions than answers. But something told him they were getting closer. And that wasn't always a good thing.

As the others began packing up, Wyatt's gaze drifted back to Kevin and Bridget. Kevin was staring at the ground, lost in thought, while Bridget hugged Pickles to her chest, her face tight with worry. Whatever secret they were keeping, Wyatt was sure it wasn't going to stay hidden for long.

And neither would his.

CHAPTER TWENTY-EIGHT

"Definitely male," Wyatt said, rubbing the back of his neck as he leaned against the wall, his shadow stretching across the squad room in the fading afternoon light. "Probably mid-thirties, give or take. But here's the kicker—John Dudley said there were scraps of fabric with the body. Decayed, but it looks like part of a suit."

"A suit?" Reese's voice cut through the quiet, sharp with disbelief. She sat perched on the edge of her desk, coffee mug in hand, her eyes narrowing as she processed the detail. "That doesn't scream accidental fall down a well to me."

"No wallet, no ID," Wyatt added, tossing a photo onto the table. "Whoever this guy was, someone went out of their way to make sure he stayed a John Doe."

Sam sat at his desk, leaning forward, arms crossed, his eyes fixed on the corkboard as if it held the answer. The room felt heavy, the weight of too many unsolved mysteries pressing down on all of them. Lucy lay quietly at his feet, her ears twitching.

"No DNA," Wyatt continued, his tone grim. "Nothing left to work with, and dental records aren't going to do us any good unless we figure out who this guy was and where he got his dental work done first. Dudley says even that's a long shot as most dentists that practiced decades ago would be retired and records purged."

Sam rubbed his jaw, the knot of frustration tightening. "No ID, no DNA, no dental records." His voice was low, measured, but there was an edge to it. "Any luck with missing persons?"

"Already started the search," Reese said, setting her mug down. "But so far, nothing that matches. It's been decades, Sam. Whoever this guy was, someone went to a lot of trouble to erase him."

Wyatt pointed to the photo on the table, his expression grim. The faded pinstripes on the deteriorated fabric were just visible, a faint echo of what must have once been an expensive suit. "Dudley's best guess? This guy was dressed to impress—probably someone important or at least someone trying to look the part."

Sam studied the image, his mind flashing back to a conversation with Mick months ago. Late-night talks about White Rock's buried secrets, the whispers that never made it past the town line.

"Mick mentioned something once," Sam said, sitting back in his chair. "A reporter. Tommy Callahan. Went missing twenty, maybe thirty years ago. Rumor was, he was digging into something big. Corruption, land deals, maybe even Convale. But he vanished, and the story went with him."

Reese straightened, her curiosity piqued. "A reporter? Disappearing in White Rock? What was he looking for?"

"That's the thing," Sam said, his gaze shifting to the whiteboard. "Nobody knows. But Mick said Callahan was onto something. Something someone didn't want getting out."

"Sounds like a motive to me," Wyatt said, crossing his arms. "If this is him—and that's a big if—it means somebody wanted that story buried. Literally."

"Could explain Garvin," Reese added, her voice thoughtful. "If Callahan's investigation tied into something Garvin stumbled onto, it could've put him in the crosshairs too."

Sam nodded slowly. It made sense. Garvin had been poking around, digging into land records, properties, boundaries—the kind of work that could uncover secrets no one wanted found.

"Garvin was looking into the property where Jo's cottage is," Sam said, his tone sharper now, the pieces clicking into place. "The land around it. Convale owns a lot of it. If Callahan was onto something back then, maybe Garvin was getting close to the same truth now."

"Which means it's still dangerous," Kevin said, his voice tense. He'd been quiet until now, his eyes fixed on the photo. "If someone killed Callahan back then, they'd have no problem doing the same to Garvin. Or anyone else who gets too close."

The room fell into a heavy silence, each of them lost in their own thoughts. Lucy stirred at Sam's feet, her ears pricking up as if sensing the tension in the air. Major leapt down from the filing cabinet, landing gracefully before padding to the door, his tail flicking dismissively.

Wyatt broke the quiet first. "I saw Marnie leave Beryl's house with that envelope. She took it straight to Parker Studies. What if Convale's using that place for something off the books? And Garvin found out?"

Reese folded her arms, her expression darkening. "Beryl's always in the middle of something shady. I don't trust her as far as I can throw her."

Sam leaned back in his chair, his gaze drifting to the whiteboard again. Beryl Thorne. Marnie Wilson. Convale Energy. The names circled in red ink felt like a noose tightening around the truth.

"We press Beryl," Reese said, her tone firm. "She's protecting herself, but she knows more than she's letting on."

Sam's jaw tightened. Beryl was a problem. She always had been. And confronting her meant more than just digging for answers—it meant dealing with the past he and Mick had spent years trying to bury. But he couldn't avoid her forever.

"I'll pay her a visit," Sam said finally. "But first, I want more on Parker Studies. What exactly is going on there?"

"I'll dig deeper," Wyatt offered.

"Good," Sam said, glancing at the clock. "Let's call it for now. Fresh eyes tomorrow."

The team began gathering their things, the tension in the room easing slightly as they prepared to leave. But Sam lingered, his eyes fixed on the photo of the suit pinned to the whiteboard.

A man in an expensive suit, dumped in a well. A reporter chasing the truth. An old man murdered. A missing bronze statue.

Whoever thought they could bury their secrets had made a mistake.

Sam didn't intend to let them get away with it.

CHAPTER TWENTY-NINE

The flickering glow from the stone fireplace filled the cozy space of Sam's cabin, casting warm shadows on the log walls. The cabin was small but homey, nestled on the outskirts of White Rock, where the pine trees pressed in close, giving it a sense of seclusion. The air inside carried the faint scent of pine and burning wood, mixing with the rich aroma of beer. It was a place built for quiet and solitude, though tonight, it buzzed with conversation.

Sam leaned back in his worn leather armchair, his fingers absently rubbing Lucy's ear as she sat beside him, ever alert. The German Shepherd's tail thumped gently against the wooden floorboards, her head tilted in that curious way, as if she was also taking in the conversation between Sam and Mick. On the coffee table in front of them, two beers sat, condensation trailing down the sides of the bottles.

"You sure about this?" Mick asked, eyebrows knitting together as he leaned forward, his own beer untouched. "You think the skeleton in the well might be that reporter I told you about years ago?"

Sam took a slow pull from his bottle of Mooseneck Ale, the local brew he favored. "That's what it's starting to look like. Missing reporter, unmarked grave, skeleton turning up after decades... The timelines match."

Mick leaned back, rubbing the stubble on his jaw as he absorbed Sam's words. "That was a long time ago, Sam. The guy just disappeared. Never found a body. People wrote it off as him skipping town after the story he was working on ruffled the wrong feathers."

"What kind of story was he working on again?" Sam asked, his gaze shifting to Lucy as she quietly padded across the room to her usual spot by the fire. She circled once then lay down, keeping one eye on the door like she always did.

Mick chuckled, his eyes following the dog for a moment before refocusing on Sam. "Oh, it was something big. A real bombshell exposé on Convale Energy. You know how it goes—corporate greed, environmental destruction, all that." He took a sip of his beer, savoring it. "The reporter, Tommy Callahan, was digging into some illegal dumping Convale was doing. Supposedly, they were dumping waste into a stream running through White Rock, contaminating the water."

Sam frowned, his mind churning. "The stream that runs behind Jo's cottage?"

Mick nodded, raising his eyebrows. "Yeah, that's the one. Funny thing, though—Garvin owned that property back then, didn't he? That's where Callahan was snooping around before he disappeared."

Sam sat up straighter, leaning forward. "You think Garvin was involved? Maybe he knew about the dumping and was part of it? Could be why he never sold the land."

Mick's eyes narrowed as he considered it. "It would make sense. If Garvin was involved or even just knew too much, it would explain why he was always so reluctant to sell the land. But it doesn't seem that way from his actions. He wouldn't be looking into the property and getting maps at the town hall; he'd already know."

The sound of Lucy's tail thumping against the floor caught their attention. She was sitting up now, alert, staring at Mick with those sharp, intelligent eyes.

It was as if she knew the conversation was getting heavier.

"I don't know, Mick," Sam said, rubbing his temples. "There's a lot we don't know yet. But if Garvin had stumbled across some evidence that could hurt Convale, that might have been the motive for his murder."

Mick nodded slowly, taking another swig of beer. "Could be that's why Callahan was sniffing around there in the first place. If he found something damning, something that could have blown the whole thing wide open, maybe that's why he ended up dead too."

Sam exhaled sharply, his fingers tightening around the neck of his bottle. "So, we've got two bodies—one in the well, the other fresh—and both might be tied to Convale's dirty dealings. That's a hell of a lot of secrets for one piece of land."

Mick shook his head. "Small towns, man. They've always got the deepest secrets."

A comfortable silence settled between them as they let the implications sink in. The fire crackled softly, and Lucy settled back down by Sam's feet, her ears twitching every so often as the wind howled against the cabin windows.

After a few moments, Sam glanced at Mick, his

voice softer. "How's Jo holding up? Have you guys come up with anything?"

Mick raised a brow, a smirk tugging at the corners of his mouth. "Jo? You know she's a pro. She's not letting this suspension get to her. We've been working some angles... but nothing really solid. Naturally, we'd share with you if we came up with anything."

"Of course. I'm sharing my info with her too." Sam leaned back in his chair, the fire's warmth taking the edge off the chill outside. But Mick, ever observant, didn't miss the way Sam's jaw clenched slightly or the way his gaze drifted to the window, as if he was looking for something—or someone.

Mick chuckled quietly, shaking his head. "Didn't know you were so worried about her."

Sam shot him a look but said nothing, the unspoken tension hanging in the air. He took another long sip of his beer, hiding behind the bottle, while Mick watched with an amused glint in his eyes.

"Look," Mick continued, leaning forward, "Jo's tough as nails. She's handling it just fine. Wouldn't surprise me if she cracks the case before you do."

Sam laughed. "Well, she does have the benefit of knowing what I know. I updated her earlier on the findings on that note she found and what we know about the skeleton so far."

Mick nodded. "I know. She said she's going to Garvin's funeral to size up the suspects—his kids."

"Yep, I'll be curious to see her take on that." Sam sighed, running a hand through his hair. "Just doesn't sit right with me, her being sidelined like this. She's got skin in the game."

"Sounds like she's only officially sidelined. She's still working the case for all intents and purposes." Mick raised his bottle in a mock toast. "To Jo, always playing it her way."

Sam clinked his bottle against Mick's and took a sip, though his mind was still on Jo. Mick's subtle smile hadn't gone unnoticed, and Sam knew the PI had picked up on something he hadn't quite admitted to himself.

Outside, the wind howled louder, and Lucy shifted, her ears pricking up again. Sam reached down, patting her head, grateful for her constant, steady presence.

CHAPTER THIRTY

The cold winter air bit at Bridget's skin as she stepped onto the porch. The trees surrounding Jo's cottage stood still, bare branches scraping against each other in the wind. The world felt eerily quiet, like it was holding its breath. She could see her own breath in front of her, little wisps that dissolved into the darkness.

Jo had left the door to the house open. She crouched just inside, holding a small piece of leftover chicken out toward Pickles, who was stubbornly perched on the edge of the porch. His fur was puffed up against the cold, and he eyed Jo suspiciously.

"Come on, Pickles. I would think after you ended up in a well, you'd welcome staying inside," Jo murmured, holding the chicken out further. The orange cat sniffed it but stayed put, his tail flicking dismissively.

Bridget shifted, glancing around at the dark woods surrounding them. The thought of Pickles wandering around in the cold with someone dangerous possibly lurking nearby made her uneasy. She tucked her hands into the pockets of her hoodie, the chill creeping in from the cold porch floor.

"I still think we should just carry him inside," Bridget muttered, eyeing the cat. "It's freezing out here, and with everything going on—"

Jo straightened, shaking her head. "No, it has to be his idea. Otherwise, he won't like being in there and will run off at the first chance. For now, he's enjoying being difficult."

Bridget gave a short laugh, but her unease remained.

Jo turned to her, brushing a strand of hair away from her face, her expression tight. "I heard from Sam today," she said. "They got the results on the note."

Bridget's heart thudded faster as Jo's words hung in the cold air. "And?"

Jo sighed, a cloud of her breath visible in the dim porch light. "No prints. No DNA. Of course. Whoever left it knew exactly what they were doing."

Bridget swallowed hard, her chest tightening. Of

course there was nothing. She hadn't expected anything different, but hearing it made everything feel that much more real—that much more dangerous.

Jo looked out into the night, her eyes narrowing slightly. "I don't want to wait around for them to make the next move."

Bridget frowned, feeling a cold knot settle in her stomach. "What do you mean?"

Jo turned back to her, folding her arms across her chest. "I think if they *thought* I wasn't here, they'd come back. Maybe leave another note. This time, I'd be secretly waiting for them and could catch them in the act."

Bridget stiffened, a wave of anxiety crashing over her. "Jo, you can't be serious. What if it's not just a note next time?"

Jo shrugged, but her jaw was set, the determination clear on her face. "I'm not just going to sit around and let them mess with me, Bridge. If I can draw them out, maybe I can figure out who they are."

Bridget's throat tightened. *You're not the one they want.* The words echoed in her mind, over and over, louder than anything Jo was saying. But she couldn't bring herself to say them. She couldn't tell Jo the truth —not yet. But what if the note wasn't about Jo at all? What if the danger was meant for her?

She glanced down at Pickles, his eyes now squinting against the cold wind. What if this person had put him in the well on purpose? Anyone who would do that to a small cat might do worse things to a human.

Jo exhaled, the frustration in her movements clear. "Look, Bridge, this could get dangerous. You should stay at a motel for a few days. Just until I figure this out."

Bridget's eyes snapped up to meet Jo's. "You want me to leave?"

Jo nodded, her gaze softening. "Just for a few days. There's someone running around out there, leaving notes—and for all we know, they put Pickles in the well. I don't want you in the middle of this. I'll pay for the room; it's no big deal."

Bridget felt a flash of panic. Leave Jo alone? Here? When there was someone out there leaving threats? Jo might be ready to risk her own safety, but Bridget couldn't walk away. She couldn't let anything happen to her sister.

"No," Bridget said, shaking her head, her voice firmer than she expected. "I'm not going anywhere."

Jo's brow furrowed. "Bridge, it's for your own safety."

Bridget shook her head again, more forcefully this

time. "You don't even have your service gun anymore, Jo. What are you going to do if someone shows up? Talk them into giving up? No way I'm leaving you here by yourself."

Jo's expression darkened, but Bridget didn't stop. "If you're staying here, then so am I. I'm not going to some motel while you put yourself in danger."

A tense silence stretched between them, and Bridget could feel Jo weighing her options. The fire in her sister's eyes hadn't dimmed, but there was something else there now—surprise, maybe? Or something else.

Finally, Jo sighed. "All right, but I don't want you getting involved if things go sideways."

Bridget bit her lip, fighting the urge to mention the gun she kept hidden under her bed. She couldn't bring it up now, but knowing it was there gave her a small sense of control—a way to protect them both.

Jo stepped back toward the door, and Bridget followed, the air between them still thick with unspoken tension. She glanced back at Pickles, still sitting on the porch, his fur ruffled by the cold wind.

"Pickles, come on," Jo called, but the cat ignored her completely. With a sigh, she opened the door, and they both stepped inside, leaving the stubborn cat to keep watch on the porch.

The warmth of the house hit Bridget immediately, the faint smell of rosemary and garlic still lingering in the kitchen. Jo walked past her and went straight to the fish tank on the side table, dropping a few flakes into the water for Finn.

"I'll keep the porch light on," Jo said, her back to Bridget, her voice softer now. "To deter anyone from going in there."

Bridget watched as Finn's orange scales shimmered under the light, her thoughts swirling. She couldn't shake the feeling that everything was closing in. She needed to talk to Kevin. Maybe he could help her make sense of all this. But for now, she had to keep Jo safe. No matter what.

Bridget stood her ground, arms crossed, as the tension in the air settled between them. The low hum of the heater and the faint splashing from Finn's tank filled the quiet room. Jo's eyes softened, the fire in them dimming slightly.

Bridget broke the silence, her voice low. "So... what's next? If you aren't just sitting around waiting, what will you do?"

Jo hesitated for a moment, glancing out the window as if weighing her next words. "I'm going to Garvin's funeral tomorrow morning. Figured I'd pay my respects. I did like the guy."

Bridget frowned. "Is that a good idea? With everything that's going on?"

Jo shrugged. "It's not just about paying respects. Sam's going to be there too. We'll meet up afterward—he can fill me in on any updates with the case. Besides," she added with a dry smile, "I wouldn't miss seeing how his kids act. If there's any animosity or guilt, I might be able to notice."

Bridget's worry deepened, but she kept quiet, watching Jo carefully. "Just... be careful, okay? Funerals bring out all kinds of emotions. And people."

Jo offered a small, reassuring smile, though her eyes were clouded with something deeper. "I will. But don't worry about me. It's just a funeral."

Bridget bit her lip, her anxiety gnawing at her. "I'm still not going anywhere, though."

Jo chuckled lightly, heading toward the kitchen. "Didn't think you would."

CHAPTER THIRTY-ONE

S am stood at the edge of the cemetery, the crisp morning air heavy with the silence that followed funerals. The lingering scent of damp earth filled his lungs as he scanned the crowd thinning around Garvin McDaniels's grave. It wasn't an overly large gathering —Garvin had kept to himself for the most part—but his kids were here, which was all Sam really cared about.

His eyes drifted to Derek, Garvin's son, who was standing a little too stiffly near the grave. Leanne, on the other hand, was making no attempt to hide her fury. Her voice, sharp and biting, carried over to Sam despite the respectful distance he kept.

"You should have found who did this by now!" Leanne snapped at one of the younger officers standing nearby, her arms crossed tight over her chest.

Her eyes blazed, cutting through the cool air like a knife. "And that statue—why is it still missing? Do you people even know how to do your jobs? How do you lose something so valuable?"

Sam could see the officer's discomfort from where he stood, but Leanne wasn't letting up. Sam had thought she would be calmer, but grief and anger had her wound tight, like a spring ready to snap.

He shifted his weight, keeping his attention focused on Derek, who hovered behind his sister. Derek wasn't saying much, his hands shoved deep into his pockets, his shoulders hunched forward. He seemed uncomfortable but kept his head down, mumbling something to Leanne as she ranted.

Sam watched the dynamic between them with interest. Derek was the one Sam was here to observe. He'd lied about being in town, and they knew he was desperate for money, his divorce draining whatever was left of his savings. And with that missing bronze statue—a piece worth a lot of money—Sam couldn't help but wonder if Derek's silence was covering something darker. Did Derek kill his father for that statue, or was he just another grieving son trying to hold himself together?

Leanne's voice rose again, her frustration palpable. "It's been days! And we still don't know who killed him! What are the police doing? Waiting for clues to fall out of the sky?"

The younger officer stammered an apology, but it did nothing to cool her anger. "I swear," Leanne continued, her voice cracking, "if you don't find whoever did this soon, I'll—"

"Leanne, enough," Derek interrupted softly, stepping closer to her. He placed a hand on her arm, trying to pull her back. "This isn't the time."

Leanne jerked her arm away, glaring at him. "When is the time, Derek? When? After they let the case go cold? When we've lost everything, just like you did?"

Sam shifted his weight, his sharp gaze catching the way Derek winced. Leanne might be angry at the police, but Derek... Derek looked like a man carrying the weight of something else entirely. Guilt, maybe?

Jo was there too. She'd arrived separately, blending in with the small crowd and keeping her distance from the family. Sam knew she was watching like he was— taking note of every little detail, every crack in the family's facade.

Leanne stormed off toward her car, the last of the mourners dispersing behind her. Derek lingered near the grave, his gaze directed at the black hole in the earth. He seemed smaller now, his face hidden in the shadow of his coat collar.

Sam stepped back, turning toward his truck parked just outside the cemetery gates. As he approached, he heard a familiar voice call out softly behind him.

"I see you've still got Lucy keeping you company," Jo said, pulling her coat tighter around her as she stepped toward the truck. A soft smile played on her lips as she glanced into the back seat, where Lucy sat, her ears perked and her tail wagging as she noticed Jo.

"She misses you," Sam replied, opening the driver's door and letting Lucy hop out to greet Jo. The dog bounded toward her, nuzzling Jo's hand, and Jo knelt to give her a good scratch behind the ears. "Probably as much as you miss being in the squad room."

Jo chuckled, though it didn't reach her eyes. "Yeah, well, sitting on the sidelines has never been my style."

Sam gestured to the passenger side of the truck. "Got doughnuts from Brewed Awakening. If that's any consolation."

Jo grinned, already moving toward the door. "Now you're talking."

They climbed into the truck, Lucy hopping into the back seat again, where she curled up on the blanket Sam kept there. Jo immediately reached for one of the doughnuts, tearing off a piece and chewing it like she hadn't had a doughnut in months. The tension between them lightened a little, though both their minds were still on the case.

Sam's eyes flicked back to the graveyard as they ate in silence for a moment. Derek was still standing by the grave, his face tilted down, his hands at his sides. Tears streaked his face now, but it wasn't the crying that bothered Sam—it was how he seemed frozen there, almost too still, like he didn't know how to leave.

"You think it's an act?" Jo asked around a bite of her doughnut, following Sam's gaze.

Sam didn't answer right away. "Hard to tell. He's grieving, sure, but... there's something off about it."

Jo licked some sugar off her thumb. "You think he's guilty? Or just feeling the pressure?"

"I don't know," Sam admitted, his gaze never leaving Derek. "He's desperate. That much we know. The guy's drowning in debt, going through a nasty divorce, and now his dad's dead. Maybe that's all it is."

They watched Derek wipe his eyes, his head still bent toward the grave.

"I'm not convinced," Sam said, his voice low. "But I think Derek knows something more than he's letting on."

Jo brushed off her hands and folded her arms. "Maybe we push him. See what cracks."

"Maybe. But let's give him some rope. He might hang himself without us having to do a thing."

Jo sighed, her eyes lingering on the now-empty graveyard. "And Leanne?"

"She's angry, but I don't blame her. We need to find that statue. And when we do, we'll find our killer."

CHAPTER THIRTY-TWO

The police station was unusually quiet for a winter morning. Kevin sat at his desk, the faint hum of the heater in the background, tapping a pen against the edge of the table as his eyes flicked back to his screen. The station felt emptier than usual with Sam at Garvin's funeral, Wyatt out on a call about Nettie Deardorff's goat, and Reese handling some paperwork in the next room.

It was the perfect moment for Kevin to look into something that had been bothering him all morning.

He slid the two notes closer, carefully comparing them. The first note was the one left on Bridget and Jo's door, taunting, ominous in its simplicity. The second was the note that had been left on Kevin's car, warning him about the thumb drive—two seemingly unrelated messages, but now, he wasn't so sure.

His gut had been nagging at him ever since Bridget mentioned the note they'd found on the door of the cottage. What were the odds of him getting a note on his car and one showing up on Jo's door? Something didn't feel right. If these two threats were connected, the implications were terrifying. He couldn't shake the feeling that the person behind these notes knew more than they were letting on.

Kevin bent closer, eyes narrowing as he studied the handwriting on both notes under the glow of the desk lamp. The letters—sharp, precise—looked eerily similar. He leaned back, his mind racing. No... it couldn't be.

He grabbed his phone and snapped a photo of each note, pulling up a document on his computer that analyzed handwriting. His heart started to pound as the software compared the two. The results popped up on the screen almost immediately—ninety-nine percent match.

Kevin froze, his pulse quickening. Had the same person written both notes?

His fingers hovered over the keyboard as a chill crept down his spine. What did this mean? Could the person threatening him about the thumb drive be involved with Bridget's past somehow? Or did they have some connection to Jo's cottage and the skeleton in the well?

He pushed back from the desk, his mind spinning. Bridget needed to know about this. She'd been worried the note was meant for her, and now, Kevin thought she might be right. The fact that the same person had written both notes changed everything.

Kevin stood abruptly, grabbing his jacket and calling out toward Reese, who was busy in the other room. "I'm going to pop out for a bit."

Reese popped her head around the corner, raising an eyebrow. "Everything okay?"

"Yeah," Kevin said, though his voice was tight. "Just... something I need to check on."

Without waiting for her to respond, Kevin bolted for the door. The cold air slapped him in the face as he stepped outside, the brisk winter wind biting at his skin. He glanced at his watch—Bridget should still be at the bakery. If he hurried, he could catch her before the lunchtime rush.

***

KEVIN PARKED his car a block away from the bakery, the warm smell of freshly baked bread and pastries wafting through the air as he approached. The small bell above the door jingled as he stepped inside, and Kevin's eyes immediately scanned the counter for Bridget.

She was there, tying up a box of muffins for a customer. She looked... tired. The weight of the past few days had taken its toll on her. She glanced up as Kevin stepped in, and her face lit up slightly when she saw him.

"You're just the person I wanted to see," she said with a small smile, wiping her hands on her apron.

He hadn't expected her to say that, and it made his heart jump in a way that was unfamiliar—but not unpleasant. He smiled back, hoping his voice sounded steady when he replied. "Glad to hear that."

"Give me a second," Bridget added, gesturing for him to wait.

Kevin nodded, his heart still racing, and he shifted nervously by the door. His mind whirled with the urgency of the news he had to tell her, but it also warmed him that Bridget seemed genuinely happy to see him.

A few minutes later, Bridget untied her apron and waved over to her coworker before slipping out from behind the counter and walking toward him. "I'm on break. Come outside with me?"

They stepped out into the cold, the quiet street offering them privacy. Bridget hugged her arms around herself, blowing into her hands to warm them as they walked around the corner to where Kevin's car was parked.

Kevin glanced at her, his mind still on the notes but curiosity piquing as he remembered her greeting. "So, what did you want to see me about?"

Bridget sighed, the puff of her breath visible in the chilly air. "It's Jo. I'm worried she's going to do something drastic. She's convinced the note was meant for her, and she's planning to set a trap or something to try to catch whoever left it." She shook her head. "I've been thinking... I can't let her go on thinking it's all about her. I need to come clean. Tell her about my past. But I wasn't sure how or if I should. And..." Bridget hesitated for a moment, glancing up at Kevin before continuing. "I also thought I should tell her that you know about it too. I didn't want it to get awkward."

Kevin blinked, feeling a warmth spread through him despite the cold wind cutting through their coats. She'd thought of him, considered his feelings about Jo knowing he was involved. That small detail meant more to him than he expected. "I appreciate that," Kevin said, his voice softer now. "It's fine by me. In fact..."

He hesitated, knowing he was about to drop a bombshell on her. "Actually, I came here to talk to you about telling Jo something too."

Bridget frowned, curiosity flickering in her eyes. "What is it?"

Kevin took a deep breath. "I checked the handwriting on both notes—the one left on your door and the one I found on my car." He paused, watching as Bridget's expression shifted to something between confusion and apprehension. "The handwriting has a ninety-nine percent match. The same person wrote both notes."

Bridget's eyes widened, her face paling. "What? But how? How could they be connected?"

"I don't know," Kevin admitted, running a hand through his hair. "But they are. And this changes everything. Whoever left those notes knows more than we thought."

"What does this mean?"

"It means we have to come clean," Kevin said firmly. "You need to tell Jo everything—about your past, the thumb drive, all of it. She's walking into something dangerous, and if she doesn't know the full picture, she could get hurt."

Kevin was right. Jo deserved the truth. And if these

notes were connected, they were all in more danger than they realized.

Bridget bit her lip, glancing up at Kevin. "But... how do we explain the thumb drive? I don't want Jo to know about how you got it from the evidence. That's the last thing you need, getting caught up in this mess."

Kevin frowned, nodding. He hadn't quite figured that part out either. "We can't tell her everything. But... there's another way. The drive was in my bag when I got out of the hospital. That's true. And when I looked at it, I found the coordinates."

Bridget raised an eyebrow. "And then what? Jo's going to wonder why we were out there that night."

"We tell her we found the coordinates and followed them. She doesn't need to know everything. Besides," Kevin added with a small smile, "Jo doesn't exactly play by the rules all the time either. She'll understand."

Bridget considered that, her mind whirring. He was right—Jo often bent the rules when she needed to, and she trusted them both. If they gave her enough of the truth, she'd likely let the rest slide.

"You're right," Bridget said softly. "It'll be fine. We'll explain it in a way she'll accept."

Kevin nodded, relieved to see her coming around.

"I'll come over tonight. We'll tell her together. You don't have to do this alone."

Bridget looked up at him, gratitude and relief softening her expression. "Thank you. I'm really glad you're in this with me."

"Of course. We're in this together."

Bridget smiled, and for a moment, the cold around them didn't seem so biting. They had a plan now—a way forward. And tonight, they'd finally come clean.

CHAPTER THIRTY-THREE

J o sat in her car and watched as Derek McDaniels stood by his father's grave . He'd been there the whole time she'd been talking to Sam, and she was starting to wonder how long he might linger. She took out her phone and snapped a few pictures of him.

When Derek finally turned and walked toward his car, Jo's pulse quickened. As much as she'd told herself that grief was messy and complicated, something about the way Derek hung back, staring at the grave like it held more secrets than closure, made her uneasy.

As Derek's taillights flickered on and his car rolled away from the cemetery, Jo shifted her car into drive, keeping a safe distance as she followed him.

The winter air was crisp, and the early-morning

sun struggled to break through the gray clouds that hung over White Rock. Jo's breath fogged the windshield for a moment before the defroster kicked in. She tightened her grip on the wheel, her eyes fixed on the road ahead. *Where are you going, Derek?*

Derek took a turn, heading out of town. Where in the world was he going?

She'd hoped she could catch Derek visiting a pawn shop and catch him with the bronze statue. But this road led away from the shops... and toward Thorne Construction.

Derek pulled into the dusty Thorne Industries construction site sprawled across the horizon like a half-finished fortress—steel beams reaching skyward, piles of gravel and lumber scattered like discarded toys.

Jo pulled into a dirt side road, parking behind thick evergreen shrubs. She could peek through the leaves and see Derek, but hopefully, no one could see her car.

Derek himself stepped out of the car, smoothing his tie as he scanned the area. Nervous, Jo thought. He looked like a man who didn't belong and who knew it.

Her gaze shifted to the far side of the lot. There was Beryl Thorne, hard hat perched on her head. She stood near a stack of steel beams, talking to a man Jo recognized immediately: Desmond Griggs.

Jo's jaw tightened. Of course Beryl would have Griggs working for her. One of them was just as shady as the other, and Beryl had a reputation for keeping her hands clean by letting others do the digging.

Derek made his way toward them, his steps hesitant. Jo raised her phone, snapping a photo as he approached.

Beryl greeted Derek with a firm handshake, all business. Jo couldn't make out their words, but the body language said plenty. Derek was deferential, almost anxious, while Beryl exuded her usual icy confidence.

Jo shifted slightly, angling for a better view. Griggs stood off to the side, arms crossed, watching the interaction like a guard dog. He said something that made Derek glance his way, his expression tightening. Jo captured the moment, the three of them framed together in the fading light.

Derek shook his head. Beryl gestured with her hands. Whatever they were discussing, it didn't seem very friendly.

Derek headed back to his car. Griggs and Beryl exchanged a few final words before splitting up. Griggs moved toward the workers. Beryl walked back to her trailer.

Her phone buzzed in her hand. Sam.

She hesitated, glancing back at the site. There was no sign anyone had noticed her, but she wasn't about to risk it. She answered quietly.

"Yeah?"

"Hi... sounds like you're up to something?" Sam said.

"Aren't I always? I just saw something odd. Check your phone in about ten seconds."

Before he could press further, Jo hung up and sent him the photos. Then she started the car and headed toward town. She had an idea about how to prove that Derek McDaniels had been lying to them all along.

JO'S PULSE quickened as she stepped into Clara Hartwell's cluttered office, the dim light from the single desk lamp casting long shadows on the walls. Maps, blueprints, and rolled-up surveys crowded the space, giving it an air of controlled chaos. The faint smell of old paper and coffee grounds lingered in the air.

Previously, Clara had said that Derek came to the office before his father died, but she'd never shown her a picture of him to be certain. Now, she could get that certainty.

Clara, seated behind her desk and squinting at a handwritten ledger, looked up, startled but composed. "Oh, Sergeant Harris. Back again?"

Jo forced a small smile, tapping her phone to wake the screen. "I need you to take a look at something." She leaned across the desk, holding out the photo she'd snapped at the construction site. "Is this the man that came in last week about the McDaniels blueprints? Garvin's son?"

Clara leaned forward, her reading glasses perched on the edge of her nose. She studied the image, her eyes narrowing as recognition dawned. "That's him," she said, her tone definitive.

Jo felt a surge of vindication. Derek. She knew he was lying, and now she had proof.

"You're sure?" Jo pressed, her eyes locked on Clara.

Clara nodded, her hand drifting toward the desk to steady herself. "Yes, that's the man who came in asking about the blueprints for Garvin's property."

Jo exhaled slowly, satisfaction spreading through her chest. She straightened, pulling the phone back and locking the screen. "Thank you, Ms. Hartwell. You've been very helpful."

"Always happy to assist," Clara said, though her expression was tinged with unease.

Jo didn't notice. Her thoughts were already miles ahead, crafting her next steps.

Outside, the late-afternoon light was already dimming, casting long shadows across the parking lot as Jo leaned against her car. The cool air bit at her skin, but she barely felt it. She tapped Sam's number on her phone, her other hand gripping the car door.

Sam picked up on the second ring. "What's up?"

"Just left Clara Hartwell's office with that photo I took," Jo said, unable to keep the edge of triumph out of her voice. "She confirmed it. Derek was the one asking about the blueprints."

There was a pause, then Sam's voice came through, steady and cautious. "Good work. But you know I can't use that. You're on leave. I'll need to follow up and get her statement myself."

Jo sighed, frustration creeping into her tone. "I know. But you'd better move fast. Derek's lying, Sam. He's in this up to his neck."

"We'll soon find out. I happen to have him coming in in about ten minutes," Sam said.

"Excellent. Hopefully, you can get the truth out of him."

Sliding into the driver's seat, Jo placed her phone

in the console and stared out the windshield, the weight of the case pressing down on her.

She should feel triumphant. This was a solid lead, something Sam could use to pressure Derek. But the satisfaction was dulled by the nagging feeling in the back of her mind.

What's Beryl's angle in all this?

Jo drummed her fingers on the steering wheel, thinking back to everything they'd uncovered so far. Beryl had handed that envelope to Marnie, who'd delivered it to Parker Studies. And now, Derek was mixed up in the blueprints. Beryl Thorne was always in the middle of things, always finding a way to skirt accountability.

Jo clenched her jaw. She couldn't let Beryl slip through the cracks again. If Beryl was tied to Convale, to Garvin's death, to Derek's lies, then Jo needed to figure out how it all connected.

Her eyes flicked to her phone. She'd already called Sam and sent him the photo. He'd take it from here. But that didn't mean Jo was ready to sit back and wait.

Marnie took that envelope to Parker Studies.

The thought settled into her mind like a stone in still water. Jo hadn't followed up on that thread yet, but it was time. Whatever was in that envelope, whatever connection Parker Studies had to this mess, it might be the key to unraveling everything.

Jo checked the time—plenty of daylight left. Her stomach rumbled, and she realized she hadn't eaten since breakfast. She'd grab a quick sandwich and head over to Parker Studies.

CHAPTER THIRTY-FOUR

"I didn't kill him, okay?"

Derek McDaniels sat across from Sam, his hands gripping the arms of the chair so tightly his knuckles had turned white. His eyes darted nervously around Sam's office, like a man looking for an exit. The slight tremor in his voice wasn't lost on Sam, who leaned back in his chair, arms crossed, keeping his expression neutral.

"Then I need to know where you were that day," Sam said calmly. "The sooner you're clear, the sooner we can figure out what really happened to your father."

Derek swallowed hard, his gaze flicking to the window behind Sam's desk, where the winter light filtered weakly through. The room seemed to press in on him, his nerves stretched tight. He shifted in his chair. "I told you, I was back home. At a bar. O'Malley's Tavern. I'm a regular there. I bet they have surveillance footage that can prove I was there."

Sam nodded slowly, watching Derek's fidgety behavior. It wasn't only the standard nervousness of being questioned about a murder—there was something deeper, a current of fear running beneath the surface. "We'll look into that," Sam replied.

Sam leaned back in his chair, arms crossed, eyes fixed on Derek. "Your father ever talk about the bronze statue he kept?"

Derek blinked, his expression blank for a moment before recognition flickered. "Oh, that old thing? Yeah, he used to brag about it all the time. Said it was some big-deal piece of art. I always figured it was just one of those things old folks like to exaggerate about."

Sam kept his tone casual, his gaze steady. "So you didn't know it was worth a lot of money?"

Derek hesitated, scratching the back of his neck. "I mean, I guess. I never really thought about it. It's just been there, you know?"

"Do you know where it is now?" Sam asked, his voice calm but probing.

Derek shrugged, trying to look indifferent. "Probably still in the house somewhere. On the mantel, maybe?"

Sam leaned forward, his voice low. "Afraid not. It's missing. We think the killer took it."

Derek's eyes widened, his composure slipping for a second before he forced a nervous laugh. "Took it? Why would anyone want that thing?"

Sam didn't blink. "Because it was the murder weapon."

Derek paled visibly, his body stiffening. "The statue? You're saying someone used it to…" He shuddered, shaking his head.

Sam studied him closely, watching every twitch, every shift in his expression. Derek was putting on a good act, no doubt about that. The question was, was it all an act? Could he really not know anything about the statue—or his father's murder?

"I'm telling you, Chief," Derek continued, his voice shaking just enough to seem authentic, "I had no idea about any of this."

"Did you know your father was planning to change his will?"

Derek shook his head. "Not before this, no."

Sam let the silence stretch, watching Derek closely. "He was going to leave the property to an environmental trust. Not to you and your sister."

Derek's jaw tightened, and Sam saw a flicker of anger in his eyes. "That's what his lawyer said, but he never told me that."

"Would that have made you angry?" Sam asked quietly. "To find out he wasn't leaving you anything?"

Derek looked down at his hands, his leg bouncing under the desk. "I'm not gonna lie. It would've pissed me off. But I wouldn't kill him over it, all right? If he wanted to leave everything to a bunch of tree huggers, that's his business."

Sam gave a slow nod then leaned forward, narrowing his eyes slightly. "Then why did you visit the town surveyor's office?"

Derek's brow furrowed in confusion. "What?"

"You were asking about maps of all your father's land," Sam continued, his gaze fixed on Derek. "Why?"

Derek blinked, shaking his head quickly. "I didn't visit any surveyor's office."

Sam didn't buy it. He leaned in, his voice dropping slightly. "Are you sure? Or was it something Beryl asked you to do?"

Derek's leg bounced faster now, his eyes darting nervously to the door before he met Sam's gaze. "I have no idea what you're talking about. I didn't ask anyone about maps."

"I find that hard to believe, Derek. You're scrambling for money, your father's properties are valuable, and maybe Beryl offered you a way out. I think you know exactly what I'm talking about."

"I don't!" Derek snapped, his voice rising with panic. "I don't know anything about maps or surveyors or whatever the heck you're getting at."

"Then help me understand," Sam said, leaning forward, his tone sharp but measured. "Because I've got witnesses placing you here in town last week. And I know you met with Beryl Thorne after the funeral. So why don't you explain what that meeting was about?"

Derek shifted in his chair, visibly uncomfortable. "She called and asked me to meet her at that construction site. She wanted to make an offer for that piece of land my father has on River Road."

Sam raised an eyebrow, skepticism etched into his face. "And what did you say?"

"I told her I'd have to discuss it with my sister. We both own it together now."

Sam leaned back, his expression unreadable, but his mind was already racing.

Was Derek telling the truth?

Why would Beryl be interested in that land? Beryl had ties to Convale through Victor Sorrentino. And

then there was the envelope Beryl had given to
Marnie. Marnie had taken that straight to Parker
Studies.

Beryl was tangled in this mess, that much was
certain. Sam couldn't shake the feeling she was orches-
trating something, pulling strings from the shadows as
she always did. And Parker Studies—it was time to pay
them a visit. But first, he needed to verify the picture
Jo sent to Clara Hartwell and have Reese check on
Derek's alibis. Jo had asked Clara, but he needed to do
it officially.

He made a mental note to head to the surveyor's
office after he was done here. For now, he needed to
wrap this up.

Sam's gaze locked back onto Derek. "All right, you
can go."

Derek blinked, surprised by the abrupt dismissal.
"That's it?"

"For now," Sam said, standing. "But don't get too
comfortable. I'll be checking your alibi. In the meantime, if you want to change your story, feel free to give
me a call."

Derek bristled, his face tightening with barely
concealed anger. "I'm not changing anything because
it's the truth." He stood quickly, grabbing his coat.

"Good," Sam said, his tone cold. "Then you've got nothing to worry about."

After Derek left, Sam watched the empty doorway for a long moment, his thoughts churning. Was Derek truly not involved? His reaction felt genuine, but Sam had seen plenty of liars put on convincing acts before.

He glanced at the clock and grabbed his jacket. First stop: Clara Hartwell's office to confirm Jo's photo. After that: Parker Studies. It was time to start untying the knots Beryl was trying to keep hidden.

CHAPTER THIRTY-FIVE

Sam stepped into Clara Hartwell's cramped office, the smell of aged paper and dust heavy in the air. The hum of the overhead fluorescent light buzzed faintly as she looked up from her desk, her reading glasses perched low on her nose.

"Chief Mason," Clara said, setting down a stack of maps. "Didn't expect to see you today. Sergeant Harris was just here."

"Oh, right... I'm just double-checking that I have things straight." Sam pulled his phone from his pocket and scrolled to the photo of Beryl and Derek.

Clara adjusted her glasses, leaning in to examine the picture. "This is the same picture she showed me."

"It is," Sam said, keeping his tone even. "Just double-checking that this is the man that came in last week looking for maps of Garvin's land." He enlarged the image to show Derek McDaniels.

Clara squinted at the photo, her brow furrowing. "Him? Oh, no. Not him." She pointed to the back of the image, her finger landing squarely on a figure just visible near the edge. "That one. The man in the background."

Sam's eyes shifted to where she was pointing. Desmond Griggs.

His gut tightened, though he kept his face neutral. "You're sure?"

"Positive," Clara replied, straightening in her chair. "That's the man who came in asking about the blueprints. He seemed particularly interested in the property lines between Garvin's land on River Road and the adjoining parcels."

Sam nodded, slipping the phone back into his pocket. "Thanks, Clara. That's helpful."

Clara smiled faintly. "Glad to assist. Let me know if you need anything else."

"I will," Sam said, already heading for the door.

Outside, Sam paused on the steps, letting the cold air clear his head. Griggs. The man was a known troublemaker, but what the heck was he doing asking about Garvin's land? And how did he connect to Beryl

Thorne? Did he work for her? He'd been at Marnie's campaign office. How did it all tie in?

The picture was shifting. Sam replayed his earlier conversation with Derek in his mind. Maybe the son was telling the truth after all. He hadn't been the one poking around the surveyor's office. Sam would still check Derek's alibis, but now, he suspected they might pan out.

Sam exhaled sharply and headed for his car. One thing was certain—Beryl Thorne's fingerprints were all over this mess. From her meeting with Derek to the envelope she'd handed Marnie, it all circled back to her. She was the common denominator.

Sliding into the driver's seat, Sam made a mental note. Next stop: Parker Studies. Whatever Beryl had her hands in, it started there. And this time, he wasn't walking away without answers.

CHAPTER THIRTY-SIX

Jo stood in front of the side door to Parker Studies, hidden away behind a row of shrubs. The faint smell of cigarette smoke lingered in the air, the ground littered with butts, as if someone had taken a break here recently. Her hand hovered over the door handle, her heart racing.

The other two entrances to Parker Studies had been locked tight. No phone number, no website, nothing. It was as if the place didn't exist. She'd tried to dig up something—anything—before coming here. No contact information, no way to schedule a meeting. Nothing.

Her gut told her there was something off about this place. Convale Energy was tied up in all of this somehow, and whatever Parker Studies was doing here, it wasn't out in the open. It reminded her of one of those secret government facilities in the movies, the kind you weren't supposed to know about. The kind that dealt with things people weren't supposed to see.

When she'd found this side door, tucked away in the shadows, she'd been shocked to see it was slightly open. Not fully ajar but not latched either. A small twig caught underneath had kept it from closing.

Jo's hand tightened on the handle, and she hesitated for a moment. She wasn't supposed to be here.

But her instincts as a cop wouldn't let her walk away. There were answers inside this place, and she wasn't leaving until she got closer to the truth.

With a deep breath, Jo slipped through the door and into the building. She bent down to remove the twig so no one would know the door had been left open.

The inside was cold. Sterile. She paused just inside the side door, unsure of what to do next. She hadn't told Sam she was doing this. She'd left him in the dark. She was officially off the case, and the less he knew about her rule bending, the better it would be for him.

The hallway stretched out in front of her, long and

narrow, and it hit her immediately that something was weird about this place. There was no reception desk, no lobby area—just a maze of sterile corridors, all lined with white doors that were shut tight. It didn't feel like a normal business.

She paused by one of the closed doors, pressing her ear against it. Faint sounds—machines whirring, maybe? But no voices. The whole place felt wrong.

She continued down the hall, glancing over her shoulder every few steps, coming up with what she would say if someone was going to come out of one of these rooms and confront her.

That was when she heard the voices.

"...a breach?" A woman's voice, low and professional, echoed from a corridor ahead. "The door was left open longer than it should've been. We need to check the east wing."

Another voice, this one male, replied, "Make sure no one's inside. If someone's here, lock it down."

Jo's heart leapt into her throat. Breach? Were they talking about her? Her eyes darted around for somewhere to hide. Footsteps echoed down the hall, getting closer. She didn't have time to think—she spotted a door marked Restroom a few feet away and darted toward it, slipping inside.

The bathroom was small, as sterile as the rest of the building, but it offered her a place to catch her breath. She leaned against the door, trying to calm her racing heart. She was trespassing. If they caught her, she had no explanation.

Her mind whirled with the implications. Convale, Marnie Wilson, and now this place—Parker Studies. What were they hiding?

Then she heard it—a quiet shuffle behind her. A soft exhale.

Jo whipped around, eyes wide, her breath catching in her throat. Standing in the corner, his expression as shocked as hers, was Sam.

"What are you doing here?" Jo hissed, keeping her voice low.

Sam straightened, stepping out of the shadows. His mouth twitched, almost a smile, but the tension between them was unmistakable. "I could ask you the same thing," he whispered back.

Jo stared at him, her mind racing. Of course Sam would be here. He'd been working this case just as hard, but she hadn't told him she was coming here. And judging by the look on his face, he hadn't planned on her showing up either.

Before she could fire back, the footsteps outside grew louder. They were right outside the door now.

They were going to be found.

Sam moved closer, his hand lightly pressing against her arm, his breath warm on her skin. "Stay quiet," he murmured.

Jo's heart hammered in her chest as she felt him lean in closer, the air between them thick with tension. There was something about being this close to him, pressed together in the small space. She tried to focus on the danger outside, but it was impossible to ignore the heat of his body next to hers.

They didn't move, standing frozen, listening to the footsteps pass. The steps stopped just outside the door, and Jo could feel the tension in Sam's body, inches away from her own. His face was so close to hers, his breath brushing against her cheek. Her mind flashed with memories of long hours spent together on cases, the unspoken connection that had always been there.

Then the door swung open.

A security guard stepped inside, his sharp eyes taking in Sam and Jo standing awkwardly by the sinks. His gaze lingered on the pair then darted to the door as if questioning why they were both inside.

"What are you doing here?" the guard asked, his tone skeptical.

Sam straightened, recovering quickly with an easy smile. "Chief Sam Mason," he said, flashing his badge.

"This is Sergeant Harris. We're here following up on a call about a break-in."

The guard frowned, his eyes narrowing. "Break-in? We don't usually involve law enforcement for something like that. We have our own security measures."

Jo folded her arms, meeting the guard's gaze without blinking. "Well, we got a call, so here we are," she said evenly, backing Sam's play.

The guard's suspicion softened slightly. "This area's supposed to be restricted. What are you doing in the bathroom?"

"I understand. This is a bit of a sensitive facility, isn't it?" Sam asked, avoiding the question about why they were in the bathroom.

The guard nodded, his suspicion melting away. "Yeah, the research we're doing is very hush-hush—high success rate, cutting-edge treatments. But that also means other companies try to steal our protocols, so we keep everything locked down. Only staff and patients are supposed to be inside."

"Treatments?" Sam asked.

The guard frowned. "Cancer treatments."

"Of course," Sam said.

Jo exchanged a glance with Sam, her mind racing with this new information. A cancer research facility? High cure rates? This wasn't at all what she'd expected, but it raised even more questions. What did Marnie Wilson have to do with a place like this?

"You'd better come with me. We'll find out who called this in."

Sam gestured for Jo to go first, his calm demeanor unshaken, but inside, Jo could feel the tension rising. The guard was suspicious—rightly so—and they needed to be careful.

The guard escorted them down the hallway to a small room, his steps brisk, his eyes constantly flicking over his shoulder as if to catch them doing something. The visitor station was a sterile corner of the building, manned by a receptionist who barely glanced up as they approached.

"Who called for outside help with a break-in?" the guard asked her sharply.

The receptionist frowned, confused, and shook her head. "No one's mentioned anything to me."

Another guard nearby, an older man with a clipboard, chimed in. "Maybe it was Dr. Leavitt," he muttered, scratching his chin. "That guy's always complaining about security issues."

The first guard rolled his eyes but didn't press further. He turned back to Sam. "I'll need you both to sign in for the record."

Jo went straight to signing the log book, which had

all the visitors' names. A name jumped out at her. Marnie Wilson. "Marnie's been visiting here a lot, huh?" she asked, keeping her tone light. "Running a campaign and dealing with a sick family member—it's a lot for anyone."

The receptionist barely looked up, but a nurse walking by hesitated, her clipboard clutched to her chest. "Oh, Marnie's mother is doing so much better," the nurse offered brightly, eager to share. "Practically a miracle."

Jo shot Sam a quick glance, and his face stayed neutral, but she saw the flicker of realization in his eyes. "That's good to hear," he said, his voice steady.

As they stepped outside, Jo exhaled, the cold air cutting through the tension still clinging to her. She turned to Sam. "Thanks for backing me up in there."

"Let's just hope no one mentions you pretended to be here officially and I played along."

Jo grimaced. "I know. Sorry about that. It was worth it, though. Marnie's mother is here. That envelope Beryl gave her—it's gotta be about paying for her treatment. She's funding all of this."

Sam's expression hardened, his jaw tightening. "Which means Beryl isn't just involved—she's pulling the strings. And Marnie's doing her dirty work."

Jo nodded, the pieces clicking into place in her

mind. "Marnie must be desperate to keep her mother alive. But what does this have to do with Garvin's death and the land?"

"That's what we need to find out. Let's stop by Holy Spirits for a drink and figure out exactly how to do that."

CHAPTER THIRTY-SEVEN

J o nursed her Coors Light as she leaned against the bar at Holy Spirits, watching the amber glow of the stained glass windows cast a warm hue over the room. The converted church buzzed with the usual Friday crowd, but the noise felt distant. Her thoughts churned, circling everything they'd uncovered at Parker Studies.

Sam sat beside her, sipping his Mooseneck beer. He placed the bottle down with a muted thud and turned to her. "Marnie's mother being there changes things," he said, his voice low enough to blend with the hum of conversation.

Jo nodded, her fingers tracing the condensation on her bottle. "Beryl's payments weren't just about buying land or keeping her quiet. She's paying for treatment. Marnie's wrapped up in this because she's desperate."

Sam's jaw tightened. "Desperation doesn't absolve her. But it does mean we need to handle Marnie carefully."

Jo exhaled slowly, her frustration simmering just below the surface. "Right. She'll do what she has to do to get her mother treatment."

Sam frowned, his gaze narrowing. "It all points to Beryl. I don't think she'd go this far without a bigger motive. She's not just petty—she's calculating."

Jo took a long sip of her beer, letting the bitterness ground her. "So what's her endgame, Sam? What does Garvin's land have to do with all this? And why is Griggs suddenly in the mix?"

Sam's hand froze mid-reach for his beer. "Griggs," he murmured, his tone shifting.

Jo raised an eyebrow. "What about him?"

Sam leaned back, staring past her like he was piecing together a puzzle. "I saw him at Marnie's campaign office a few weeks ago. I didn't think much of it then—just assumed he was another hired hand—but when I went to question Clara Hartwell about Derek being there, she identified Griggs in the photo."

"What?"

Sam explained how he went to Clara's office so he

could have her officially identify Derek. "And when I pointed to Derek in the photo, she said not that guy... the other guy."

Jo sighed. "And the other guy in the photo was Griggs. I never specified which man I was talking about."

Sam nodded. "Griggs doesn't just show up somewhere unless there's trouble. And if he's tied to Beryl and Marnie..."

Jo's stomach twisted. "Then whatever this is, it's bigger than just land disputes or campaign favors."

Sam nodded slowly, his expression hardening. "I need to confront Beryl. If anyone knows what Griggs is up to and how it ties back to Garvin's murder, it's her."

Jo smirked faintly. "Good luck with that. You know she's going to dance around every question you throw at her."

"Maybe," Sam said, his voice steady. "But I'm not letting her walk away this time. Though maybe I should have Wyatt follow him just for good measure. Wyatt's pretty good at tailing people."

Jo felt a pang of admiration for his resolve. Sam's patience and methodical approach were a stark contrast to her own gut-driven style, but it was moments like this that reminded her why they made such a good team.

Her phone buzzed against the bar, pulling her from her thoughts. She glanced down, her stomach knotting when she saw Bridget's name and the message.

Meet me at the cottage. It's urgent.

Jo's first instinct was to tell Sam. She opened her mouth—but then stopped herself.

A cold thread of guilt coiled in her chest. Parker Studies. If anyone found out Sam had let her pretend she was there officially, it could cost him his job. And the trap she wanted to set for the note leaver at the cottage? If Sam showed up and got tangled in that, it could look like he was involved. She couldn't drag him down with her rule bending.

But as she stared at the message again, another worry gnawed at her. What if the note leaver had Bridget? What if her plan to flush out whoever was behind the threats had put her sister in danger?

Her pulse quickened, and she downed the rest of her beer, trying to push the panic down. She couldn't afford to lose her focus now.

"Everything okay?" Sam asked, catching her hesitation as he stood and slipped on his jacket.

Jo forced a tight smile, sliding her phone into her pocket. "Yeah, Bridget wants to go over something tonight. Probably garden plans or something," she lied, her voice deliberately light.

Sam studied her, his brow furrowed slightly, but he nodded. "All right. If she needs anything, you call me."

"I will," she promised, the weight of her unspoken fears pressing heavy on her chest.

Sam finished his beer. "I'm off to deal with Beryl. I'll let you know how it goes."

"Good luck," Jo said, managing a small smile.

She watched him leave, waiting until the door swung shut behind him before grabbing her coat. Her fingers brushed against her phone as she hurried outside, her heart pounding.

Bridget's message replayed in her mind like a warning bell. If the note leaver had Bridget, she'd never forgive herself.

CHAPTER THIRTY-EIGHT

J o pulled into the driveway, her truck's headlights sweeping across the porch. Her chest tightened at the sight of Kevin and Bridget sitting on the steps with Pickles stretched out lazily beside them. The tension in their posture sent a ripple of unease through her.

She barely killed the engine before stepping out of the car. "What's going on?" Jo asked, her boots crunching against the gravel as she hurried up the steps. Her eyes darted from Kevin's somber expression to Bridget's faintly guilty one. "What's wrong? Is everything okay?"

"Everything's fine," Bridget said quickly, too quickly. She glanced at Kevin, who gave her a slight nod. "But we have something we need to tell you."

Jo raised an eyebrow, folding her arms. "I'm listening."

Kevin stood and gestured toward the front door. "Maybe we should go inside for this."

Jo's unease deepened. She followed them into the living room, where the warmth of the cottage clashed with the knot forming in her stomach. Bridget hovered near the arm of the couch, fidgeting, while Kevin stood near the fireplace, his hands in his pockets.

"All right," Jo said, breaking the silence. "What's this about?"

Kevin exhaled and pulled a folded piece of paper from his jacket pocket. "This."

Jo unfolded the note, her breath catching as she read the familiar blocky handwriting.

Secrets always come out.

Her eyes snapped to Kevin. "This... This is similar to the one on my door. Where did you get this?"

Kevin hesitated, glancing at Bridget before answering. "I found it on my windshield a few days ago. Before you found yours."

Jo's brow furrowed. "Why would someone leave this for you?"

Kevin shifted uncomfortably. "Because of the thumb drive."

Jo stared at him. "Thumb drive?"

Kevin looked down. "When I got out of the hospital, they gave me a bag with things in it, and a thumb drive was in there. I had no idea what it was from."

Jo's gaze narrowed. "And you didn't think to tell anyone about this?"

Kevin winced. "I didn't know what it was at first, and I was embarrassed because of my memory issues. I thought it was blank or just junk. But then..."

He glanced at Bridget again, as if seeking permission, and she nodded slightly.

Kevin continued, "When I was on evidence room duty, recovering, I found this old notebook in the evidence room, tied to one of Lucas Thorne's narcotics cases. There were these weird codes scribbled in the margins, and on a hunch, I tried one on the encrypted part of the thumb drive."

Jo was all ears. She didn't blame Kevin for holding back about the thumb drive. She understood how hard his memory issue had been and how much he'd worked to recover. Besides, she'd done things much worse. "And it worked?"

Kevin nodded. "There were numbers that looked like GPS coordinates. Those led us to that field behind Hazel Webster's house."

Jo blinked, her mind spinning. "Wait. You mean...

that's how you two just happened to be there the night Hazel grabbed me?"

"Yes," Bridget said quietly, stepping closer. "But Kevin didn't tell anyone because he was already worried about keeping the drive. He didn't mean for it to go this far, Jo. He was—"

Jo held up a hand, stopping her. "You thought I'd be mad?" She laughed, the tension in her chest easing slightly. "Kevin, Sam and I have bent the rules more times than I can count. You don't need to hide stuff like this from me. But what does this have to do with what's going on now?"

Kevin's expression darkened. "The notes." He gestured to the one Jo still held. "The handwriting matches. Whoever's leaving these knows about the thumb drive and whatever's tied to it."

Jo looked between them, her mind racing. "And you think... what? That something's still out there? The FBI dug that place up. Wouldn't they have found it?"

"Maybe not," Kevin said. "If it was buried deep enough, they wouldn't have gone that far. Think about it—if whoever left these notes is desperate enough to connect the thumb drive to Garvin's case, there's something out there they don't want anyone to find."

Jo's grip on the note tightened, the weight of his

words settling over her. "All right," she said, her voice firm. "We're going back to that field."

Before they moved, Bridget cleared her throat, drawing Jo's attention.

"There's something else," Bridget said, her voice hesitant.

Jo turned to her, raising an eyebrow. "What is it?"

Bridget hesitated, glancing down at her hands. "When the note was left on our door, I thought it was for me."

Jo froze, her chest tightening. "For you? Why would you think that?"

Bridget took a deep breath, meeting Jo's eyes. "Because of my past. Before I came here... I wasn't exactly living on the right side of the law. I ran with a crew. We pulled jobs—small ones, mostly. But one wasn't so small. Someone got killed. Anyway, I got out, but I'm worried someone from back then might be looking for me."

Jo stared at her, the weight of the confession hitting like a punch. "Bridget... why didn't you tell me this before?"

"I didn't want to drag you into it," Bridget said, her voice cracking slightly. "You've done so much for me, Jo. I didn't want to ruin the life I've built here—or worse, put you in danger."

Jo's gaze softened, and she reached out, gripping Bridget's hand. "Bridget, we're in this together. All of us."

Kevin nodded, his voice steady. "That's why we came to you, Jo. This isn't just about the thumb drive or the notes anymore. It's all connected—Garvin's murder, the body in the well, Convale. Whatever's hidden at those coordinates could blow this whole thing wide open."

Jo stood, determination hardening her features. "Then let's not waste any more time."

Bridget and Kevin exchanged a look before grabbing their jackets. As they stepped out into the cold night, Jo's mind was already racing ahead. Whoever had gone to such lengths to hide the truth was about to have their secrets dragged into the light.

CHAPTER THIRTY-NINE

Sam parked his truck at the edge of the construction site. He glanced at the lights on in the rusted trailer ahead, the temporary office for Thorne Construction, and felt the familiar weight of frustration settle in his gut. When Beryl hadn't been home, he'd come here, hoping she was working late. Lucy sat beside him in the passenger seat, her ears perked, her posture stiff, her dark eyes fixed on the trailer.

"You don't like it here either, huh?" Sam muttered, giving Lucy a quick scratch behind the ears. "Can't say I blame you."

Lucy huffed softly, her nose twitching as she looked toward the trailer. She seemed reluctant to go inside, and Sam didn't blame her. Every interaction he had with Beryl Thorne felt like walking through a field of land mines.

"Hopefully, this will be quick," Sam said, though he didn't really believe it.

He climbed out of the truck, Lucy hopping down after him, her tail low but alert. As they approached the trailer, the cold wind bit at Sam's face, a reminder of the winter chill that never seemed to leave White Rock.

Sam knocked on the metal door, the sound echoing sharply across the construction site. A moment later, the door creaked open, and there stood Beryl Thorne, a smirk already tugging at the corners of her lips.

"Sheriff," Beryl drawled, leaning against the door-frame with her arms crossed. "To what do I owe the pleasure?"

Sam met her gaze evenly. "Garvin McDaniels's murder."

Beryl's smirk widened, though her eyes held no humor. "Murder? What would I know about that?"

Sam stepped forward, the wind picking up behind him. "You tell me, Beryl. You've been meeting with his son."

For a split second, something flickered across Beryl's face—something she quickly masked with a nonchalant shrug. "Derek? Sure, I've spoken to him.

He's broke. What's the harm in listening to someone trying to sell their daddy's property?"

Sam didn't move, didn't blink. "I'm more interested in why you're interested."

Beryl's smirk deepened, and she pushed the door open wider. "Come on in, Sheriff. Let's talk."

Beryl settled behind her desk and looked up at Sam. Lucy chuffed as if to say "Let's get out of here."

"You know as well as I do, Sam, we've got bigger problems than Garvin's murder."

Beryl Thorne's voice was cold, each word clipped as she tapped a pen against the open ledger on the desk in front of her. Her gaze was steely, almost daring Sam to challenge her. The cramped trailer smelled faintly of coffee and motor oil, with piles of paperwork scattered across the small table where Beryl sat.

Sam stood just inside the door, arms crossed, his expression tight. Lucy sat obediently at his side, ears still perked up but silent. Sam could feel the tension between them, thicker than the cigarette smoke that lingered faintly in the air. He'd been prepared for Beryl's usual stonewalling, but this... This was something new.

"Bigger problems?" Sam asked, his voice carefully measured. "You're telling me there's something bigger than the murder of a man like Garvin McDaniels?"

Beryl's eyes flickered with amusement, a cold smile curling at the corners of her mouth. "Lucas."

At the mention of Lucas Thorne, Sam's pulse quickened. He had almost forgotten how dangerous that name could sound coming out of Beryl's mouth. Lucas, sitting in prison for his crimes, was still a looming shadow over everything. And now, Beryl was bringing him up?

"Lucas is still in jail," Sam said, his voice flat. "And that's where he's staying."

"Not for long," Beryl shot back, her voice icy. "His appeal is about to be approved. And when he walks out of that courtroom, I want you to remember this conversation, Sam, because if he gets out of jail, it's not going to be good for you."

Sam's jaw tightened, his fists clenching at his sides. "You think I have any control over that? Lucas is in prison because he belongs there. The law decides if he stays or goes."

Beryl's laughter was sharp, cutting through the tension like a blade. "Oh, don't play dumb, Sam. You and I both know the law can be... flexible. You've bent it before. And I'm telling you now, if Lucas walks, you'll regret it. I have a way of knowing things that you don't want getting out."

The warning hung in the air like a noose tightening around his neck. Sam didn't flinch, but inside, anger burned hot. He didn't want to think about the past Beryl was hinting at. Not now. Not with everything else on the line.

He exhaled slowly, reining in the fire that threatened to erupt. "I didn't come here to talk about Lucas, Beryl. What do you know about Garvin McDaniels?"

Beryl's expression shifted, growing guarded as she leaned back in her chair. "Garvin was a stubborn old man. He was sitting on prime land, and I made him a fair offer. Simple as that."

"I'm not talking about land deals," Sam said, his voice low, edging toward frustration. "I'm talking about his murder."

Her lips curled into a smirk. "You think I had something to do with it?"

"I think you've got more connections than you let on," Sam replied, meeting her gaze without blinking. "You and I both know you had a conversation with Derek McDaniels. And it wasn't just about the property, was it?"

At that, Beryl rolled her eyes, dismissive. "Oh, please. Derek came to me. He's broke, and his daddy wasn't about to leave him a penny. He was looking for a way out. I just showed interest in buying the land, like any good businesswoman would."

"And you didn't try to bribe him?" Sam asked, watching her closely.

Beryl let out a soft laugh, waving her hand dismissively. "Bribe him? For what? I don't need to bribe a man who's already drowning in debt. He would have sold to me eventually. I was just waiting for the right moment. The idea of me bribing him is absurd."

Sam studied her for a moment, searching for any cracks in her facade. Beryl was smooth—too smooth. But her casual tone and lack of hesitation were enough to make him doubt Derek's version of the story. Still, there was something off here. Something that didn't sit right.

"And Marnie Wilson?" Sam pressed. "What's going on between the two of you?"

For the first time, Beryl hesitated, her expression tightening. She glanced away briefly before meeting his gaze again, her eyes sharper now. "Marnie? We're acquaintances. Friends, if you can call it that. I supported her campaign, just like any other concerned citizen would."

Sam didn't buy it. He remembered Wyatt's report. The envelope he'd seen Marnie carrying from Beryl's office couldn't have just been a campaign contribution. Sam had a creeping suspicion that Marnie was involved in something deeper than a mayoral race. "Friends, huh?" he asked, his tone skeptical.

Beryl's eyes narrowed. "What are you getting at?"

"Just curious," Sam said, shrugging lightly, though his gut told him there was more to dig into. "If you're just acquaintances, then why are her name and yours tangled up in all this mess?"

Beryl's smile faded, replaced by a cold, unreadable look. "You're barking up the wrong tree, Sam. Marnie and I have nothing to do with Garvin's murder. If you're smart, you'll focus on the real threats."

Sam held her gaze for a long moment, weighing his next words carefully. He knew he wasn't going to get much more out of her—not now, anyway. But he'd be back. He wasn't done with Beryl Thorne, not by a long shot.

"Thanks for your time, Beryl," Sam said finally, his voice edged with sarcasm as he stood. "I'll be in touch."

CHAPTER FORTY

The old dirt road twisted through the woods like a scar, rutted with years of neglect. Kevin's truck bumped along the uneven terrain until the path narrowed to little more than two tire tracks swallowed by grass and underbrush. Jo leaned forward, gripping the dashboard, her eyes scanning the dense forest pressing in on either side.

"This is it." Kevin pulled the truck to a stop. The engine cut out, and the quiet of the woods rushed in. Jo climbed out first, her boots crunching in the snow.

The land ahead was a mess. Large swathes had been dug up, the ground churned and scarred by bulldozers during the FBI's investigation of the Webster property. Piles of loose dirt and clay were scattered around like forgotten monuments to a gruesome past.

"This place gives me the creeps," Bridget muttered, stepping out and crossing her arms against the chill in the air.

Jo nodded. She couldn't blame her. The memories of what had been unearthed here lingered like the stench of old secrets refusing to fade. And it still left a hole that the body of their sister, abducted all those years ago, wasn't one of the ones found. "At least we'll be able to dig. The ground would be frozen if not for being recently disturbed."

Kevin grabbed three shovels from the back of the truck and handed one to Jo and another to Bridget. "You think we should call Sam?" he asked as they started toward the woods.

Jo paused, weighing the decision. "Not yet. Might be better if he doesn't come out. We wouldn't want anyone to think he's letting me investigate while I'm suspended. Let's find out if anything's here first, then we'll call him."

Bridget glanced around nervously, her eyes darting toward the tree line. "I don't like this, Jo. What if whoever left those notes is watching us right now?"

Jo rested a hand on Bridget's arm, her voice calm but firm. "Stay close. We're not splitting up. If anything feels off, we leave."

They moved carefully across the uneven ground,

stepping over deep grooves and patches of overturned soil. Kevin checked the GPS app again, adjusting their path slightly to the west. The coordinates led them to a small clearing where the ground had been freshly dug and partially refilled.

"Right here." Kevin stabbed his shovel into the ground, the blade slicing through the soft dirt with ease. Bridget and Jo followed, their movements swift and methodical. The scent of damp earth filled the air as they worked in silence, each shovelful revealing more of what lay hidden beneath.

Kevin grunted as his shovel hit something hard. "I think we've got something."

Jo dropped to her knees, brushing dirt away with her hands. A metallic edge glinted in the faint light filtering through the trees.

"It's a box," Kevin said, excitement creeping into his voice.

Bridget leaned in and pulled the box out. It was a stainless steel document box. Her fingers found the latch and pried it open with a sharp *snap*. She hesitated for a moment, then she lifted the lid.

The contents were preserved despite the years underground. Jo reached in carefully, pulling out a worn leather wallet. She flipped it open, revealing an ID card.

"Tommy Callahan," she murmured, reading the name aloud.

Bridget stepped closer, her voice uncertain. "Callahan? That's... the skeleton in the well?"

Jo nodded slowly, her mind racing. The implications hit her like a punch to the gut. "That's him. The reporter Mick told us about. The one who disappeared decades ago."

Kevin leaned on his shovel, his face tight. "But what's his wallet doing here, in this box, buried on the Webster property? This box has to be as old as he is."

"Decades," Jo agreed, her voice quiet but firm. "Which means whoever killed him put his wallet here on purpose."

"Trying to send a message, maybe?" Kevin asked.

"To who? I don't think anyone else dug this up before us," Jo said.

"Maybe someone put it here to gain some sort of leverage, but they never needed to use it," Bridget suggested.

"Or were killed and couldn't use it," Kevin said.

Jo rifled through the rest of the box, pulling out a small stack of photographs. One of them was a surprise. It showed an image of a young Beryl Thorne shaking hands with a man Jo didn't recognize. Another photo showed Beryl near what looked like a construction site.

"This connects Beryl to something," Jo said, her voice tinged with disbelief.

"To what?" Kevin asked.

"I'm not sure, but it must be something important," Jo said.

"And something someone wouldn't want anyone to see," Bridget added.

Jo's mind raced ahead to the implications of what they'd found as she closed the box.

She stood, brushing dirt from her hands. "Now, it's time to call Sam."

Kevin straightened, glancing toward the trees. "We should get out of here first. This place doesn't feel right."

CHAPTER FORTY-ONE

S am stood at Jo's door, tension settling in his shoulders. She'd called, said she had something to show him, but hadn't given any details. Beside him, Lucy waited, alert, as if she could sense the unanswered questions hanging in the air. Jo opened the door, her expression a mixture of excitement and worry. But it wasn't only Jo's expression that caught him off guard—it was the presence of Kevin sitting on the couch, his posture rigid, with Bridget leaning forward beside him.

"Kevin," Sam said, stepping into the warmth of the cottage and shutting the door behind him. "Didn't expect to see you here."

Kevin gave him a nod, his expression unreadable.

Lucy trotted in and made a beeline for Kevin, her tail wagging.

"Lucy," Jo said, scratching behind the dog's ears briefly before motioning to the coffee table.

Sam's gaze shifted to the stainless steel box sitting on the table. It looked ordinary enough, but the way everyone was looking at it told him it was anything but. He unbuttoned his coat and approached, his eyes darting between Jo and Bridget. "Is this what you called me about?"

Jo gestured for him to sit, her tone businesslike. "We dug it up at the coordinates linked to a thumb drive Kevin has. And before you ask—I didn't call you before we went because I didn't want you tied to it officially."

Sam sank into the armchair, eyeing the box warily. "Thumb drive?"

They took turns explaining how Kevin had come into possession of the thumb drive and had figured out the code to get the coordinates.

Bridget leaned forward, her voice firm. "Kevin got a note on his car, same handwriting as the one left on Jo's door. We think this box and the skeleton in the well are related to Garvin's murder somehow."

Kevin stood, grabbing the box and flipping the latch. "Inside is what changes everything." He opened it, revealing its contents: an old leather wallet, a stack of grainy photographs, and some documents Sam couldn't quite make out.

Jo picked up the wallet and handed it to him. "The skeleton in the well? This ID belonged to him. Tommy Callahan."

Sam's stomach tightened as he flipped the wallet open, his eyes scanning the faded license. "So Callahan was digging into something he wasn't supposed to, and someone made sure he stayed quiet."

"Exactly," Jo said, her tone clipped. "And it all goes back to Convale somehow."

Sam set the wallet down and sifted through the stack of photos, frowning as he flipped through them. One image froze him.

It was *Beryl Thorne.*

Younger, maybe in her late twenties, standing beside a man Sam didn't recognize. She was at what looked like a construction site—wearing a sharp blazer and a hard expression that didn't match the picture of an innocent housewife she'd painted.

"Is this..." Sam started, holding the photo up so the others could see.

"A young Beryl," Jo confirmed, leaning in to study the photo again. "Looks like she was involved in something back then."

Bridget frowned, her voice low and careful. "I thought Beryl took over Thorne Industries after her husband went to jail—just an innocent housewife stepping in to save the family name."

Kevin snorted, crossing his arms. "Doesn't look so innocent to me. She's right in the thick of whatever this was."

Jo's eyes narrowed, her mind clearly running at full speed. "Someone put those photos in this box for a reason. They prove something. Beryl wasn't just along for the ride—she was part of it. Maybe even the mastermind."

"And someone knew it," Jo added. "They buried the truth with Callahan, but they didn't destroy it. They locked it away—like they were saving it as insurance."

"We know Beryl Thorne is the key to Garvin's murder, but she wouldn't admit to anything when I talked to her earlier. She's in tight with Convale, and now, we know Convale is mixed up somewhere in all of this. Callahan was onto something all those years ago. This box could change the power dynamic with Beryl," Sam said.

"What about Marnie Wilson?" Jo asked.

Sam nodded. "Yep, now that we have leverage over Beryl, we can use that to get Marnie talking."

"Marnie's the weaker link. This"—Jo tapped the box lightly—"could come in handy later to keep Beryl in line."

"What about the person that left the notes?" Bridget chimed in, her voice steady but laced with concern. "They seem to know our moves. They might already know we have this."

Sam exchanged a glance with Jo. "True," he admitted. "But maybe that person wants us to have it. What if those notes weren't threats? What if they were breadcrumbs? Whoever left them might be trying to help us."

Jo frowned, leaning forward. "Or they could be playing us. Leading us right into a trap."

Kevin cleared his throat. "Either way, we don't have enough to figure out who they are yet, so I agree our next move is to see what we can get out of Marnie."

Jo leaned forward, her tone skeptical. "Marnie's shifty. She's good at wriggling out of tight spots. All we've got is that envelope from Beryl and her visits to Parker Studies. It's not enough to stick in court. We need something solid."

Sam nodded, rubbing the back of his neck. "You're not wrong. It's thin. But if we push—"

"What's this?" Bridget interrupted. She had been

quietly petting Lucy, her fingers idly brushing through the German Shepherd's thick fur. Now, her hand froze, her brow furrowing. "What's this on your tail, girl?"

Sam turned as Bridget lifted Lucy's tail, revealing a few stray hairs faintly tinged with blue underneath.

"Oh, I thought I cleaned all that off. Guess I'm not much of a cleaner," Jo said.

"What is it?" Sam asked.

"Some kind of blue paint or something. She had it on her tail at the station, before I got relieved of duty." Jo made a face.

Something clicked. "Was that right after we went to Marnie's campaign headquarters? I remember they were working on a poster for the campaign. It was blue. And Griggs was standing next to it."

Kevin's head snapped up, his expression sharp. "Wait a minute. The blue liquid at Garvin's cabin." His voice dropped into a hard edge. "The lab said it was diluted paint."

Jo's eyes widened, her mind racing. "If that's the same paint, then that ties her directly to Garvin's cabin."

Kevin grinned, the first real smile breaking across his face all night. "Now, that's solid. She can't explain her way out of that."

Sam nodded, the weight of the discovery settling over him. "You're right. But we need to test them to see if they are the same. Though Marnie doesn't need to know we haven't done that …"

"If we bluff and say they tested the same, she'll fold. Unless she's totally innocent." Jo grabbed an evidence bag. She happened to keep a stash in the drawer under Finn's tank. She carefully cut the hairs, bagged them, and handed them to Sam.

Sam stood, his decision made. "Okay, looks like we have some work to do. Including paying a little surprise visit to Beryl and Marnie. I don't think any of this can wait until tomorrow." He glanced toward Kevin. "You want to come?"

Kevin straightened, a flicker of surprise crossing his face before he nodded. "Yeah, I'm in."

Lucy let out a soft woof from her spot by the door as if sensing the shift in energy. Sam reached down to give her a quick scratch behind the ears. "Let's go."

CHAPTER FORTY-TWO

S am left Kevin at the station to submit the paint analysis request and headed to confront Beryl. He'd already decided that Kevin's presence would only make Beryl clam up. This was a conversation best handled alone.

By now, Beryl would be home. Her towering brick house loomed in the distance as he turned onto her driveway. Lights spilled onto the manicured lawn, every bulb precisely placed. The house was as calculated as its owner—intimidating, unyielding.

Sam parked and glanced at Lucy in the back seat. Her ears perked up, and she let out a low, restless whine.

"Not this time, girl," he said, closing the door behind him. He almost smiled at the dramatic huff she gave in reply. But this wasn't a moment for smiles. Beryl Thorne required every ounce of focus he had.

The brass knocker had barely sounded before the door swung open. Beryl stood there, tall and immaculately dressed, the epitome of grace under fire. Except her eyes—sharp and calculating—betrayed the irritation she didn't bother to mask.

"Chief Mason," she said coolly. "What brings you to my door at this hour? Trouble in paradise?"

Sam didn't answer, stepping inside uninvited. The icy gust of winter air followed him in. "We need to talk."

Beryl shut the door, her gaze narrowing. "And here I thought you knew how to use a phone."

Sam didn't rise to the bait. Instead, he scanned the pristine foyer, taking in the marble floors and glittering chandeliers. Everything about the place screamed untouchable wealth. But everyone had something to lose. Even Beryl Thorne.

She led him into a sitting room that felt more like a museum exhibit than a living space. Sam caught sight of a decanter of whiskey on a tray.

Beryl poured herself a whiskey, neat, and left the second glass empty. Message received.

She swirled the amber liquid in her glass. "So, why are you here?"

Sam pulled out his phone, swiping to the photo of the younger Beryl they'd found in the box. He held it up, watching her face carefully. Her reaction was subtle, but it was there—a quick tightening of her jaw, a flicker of her eyes toward the screen. Then it was gone, buried under her trademark calm.

"Where'd you find that?" she asked, her tone dismissive, but there was a faint edge to it.

"You tell me," Sam said. "It's you, isn't it? Younger, sure, but still you."

Beryl's lips curved into a faint, amused smile. "And what exactly do you think that proves?"

Sam took a step closer, his voice dropping. "I think it proves you're not just the long-suffering wife who picked up the pieces of your husband's empire. You were in the thick of it all along. Whatever game you and Lucas were playing, it didn't end with his conviction, did it?"

Beryl took her time, lifting her glass and sipping her whiskey. When she finally spoke, her voice was like silk wrapped around steel. "You don't know what you're talking about."

Sam didn't need to. He just had to make her think he did. "What I do know is that you've been holding something over my head for years. You think that gives you the upper hand." He held up the phone again, his voice hard. "This changes that."

For the first time, the mask slipped. Her knuckles whitened around the glass, just for a moment. Then she recovered, her tone icy. "If you think a photograph is going to scare me, you're more naive than I thought."

"This isn't just a photograph," Sam pressed. "This is proof of what you've been up to. You want to keep that skeleton in the closet? Fine. But if you try to use what you have on me, I'll make sure this sees the light of day."

Beryl's eyes narrowed, and for the first time, she seemed truly unnerved. "You're bluffing."

"Am I?" Sam asked, his tone flat. "You want to test me?"

The room felt colder, the weight of the standoff pressing down like a physical force. Beryl set her glass down with deliberate precision, her poker face cracking enough to show her unease.

"Fine. So it's checkmate then?" she asked, her voice quieter now, almost resigned. "Is that all you came for?"

"No, there's something else. Garvin McDaniels," Sam said. "What happened to him? What's so important about that land?"

Beryl turned to the window, one hand gripping the curtain. "How would I know?"

"Because I think you're behind it. You and your friends at Convale."

She didn't answer immediately, staring out at the dark lawn. Finally, she spoke, her voice low. "You're looking at the wrong woman."

Sam frowned. "What's that supposed to mean?"

Beryl turned back to face him, the light from the window catching in her pale-blue eyes. "It's not me you should be after. It's Marnie Wilson."

"Marnie?" he repeated.

Beryl nodded, slowly, deliberately. "Your future mayor. She's been circling that property for years. I thought Garvin was paranoid, but he was right about one thing—Marnie is dangerous. Her campaign? Funded by people who don't give a damn about White Rock."

Sam took a step closer. "Who? Convale?"

Beryl's lips curved into a faint smile. "You could say that. But Marnie isn't just taking their money. She's in deep. Everything she's done, every move she's made—it's all been about that land. Even her bid for mayor."

Sam took a step closer, his gaze locking with hers. "You're saying she's the mastermind?"

Beryl raised a single brow, her smile faint but mocking. "I'm saying you're wasting your time here when the real culprit is sitting in her campaign office, pulling strings."

Sam watched her carefully, gauging every word, every flicker of her expression. Beryl was good—too good. She wouldn't crumble under pressure, and she'd never willingly implicate herself. If she was pointing the finger at Marnie, it wasn't because she wanted justice. It was because she was hiding something.

"Why would I believe you?" Sam asked.

Beryl shrugged. "You don't have to believe me. I have proof."

But as the pieces clicked into place, a different picture emerged. The envelope from Beryl, the payments, Marnie's mother tucked away at Parker Studies—none of it screamed mastermind. It screamed pawn. Manipulated. Used.

Sam's jaw tightened as realization struck. Beryl wasn't pointing a finger at Marnie because Marnie was in charge. She was doing it because Marnie was the loose thread that could unravel everything.

"You always have proof," Sam said, his voice flat. "Convenient how it only shows up when it serves you."

Beryl's smile didn't falter. "Believe what you like.

But if you want the truth, Marnie's your next move. Don't waste time with me, Chief."

Sam didn't respond, letting the silence stretch. She'd overplayed her hand, trying to redirect him. But she'd also given him the one thing he needed: the perfect angle to push Marnie to talk.

"You think you're untouchable," Sam said finally, slipping his phone back into his pocket. "But leverage works both ways, Beryl. Don't forget that."

Her smile tightened just a fraction. A crack but not one she'd ever let him see fully. "Goodbye, Chief Mason."

Sam turned on his heel and walked out, the cold air slicing through him as he stepped onto the stone porch. Lucy waited in the truck, her nose pressed against the glass. He climbed in, giving her a quick pat as she leaned against him.

As he started the engine, his mind raced ahead. Beryl thought she'd steered him into a trap, but she'd miscalculated. And now, thanks to Beryl, Sam had what he needed to make Marnie talk.

"Let's see how much she's willing to say once she finds out you've thrown her under the bus, Beryl," Sam muttered as he drove off into the night, determination settling in his gut.

Marnie had answers. And Sam was going to get them.

CHAPTER FORTY-THREE

Kevin logged the paint analysis request, his fingers punching the keys harder than necessary. He didn't know why the system had to ask him three times if he wanted to confirm a sample.

Yes, dammit. That's why I'm here.

He leaned back, exhaling. The monitor blinked its green confirmation. Paint sample? Done.

Next up, Lucy's fur. Kevin glanced at the small plastic evidence bag beside the keyboard. Inside, the faint blue streak still clung to the hairs they'd trimmed from Lucy's tail earlier at Jo's place. Whatever it was—paint, dye, who knew—it had smeared onto her when she got too close to something.

Too late to send it to the lab tonight, but first thing tomorrow? It'd be out the door.

Kevin typed in the case file, pausing to double-check the chain-of-custody notes. His name. Sam's. All clean. Evidence logged, bag sealed, chain intact. He tapped the enter key and watched the details lock into place on the screen.

He sat back, glancing around the quiet squad room. It felt weird to be here alone. Well, not quite alone. Major, the station cat, slept sprawled across the top of a filing cabinet like he owned the place.

Kevin didn't mind the quiet. It let him think.

Sam had gone to see Beryl Thorne alone tonight. Kevin didn't know why, and he didn't need to. There was history there—anyone with eyes could see that much. Sam kept his past locked up tight, but heck, didn't they all? Kevin had his own history too. Things he didn't talk about. Things he wasn't proud of.

Sam didn't ask about any of it. And Kevin didn't ask about Beryl. That was how trust worked. You earned it, piece by piece, until it didn't matter where you'd come from—only where you stood now.

And for the first time in years, Kevin felt like he stood in the right place.

Sam hadn't even been angry about the thumb drive. He'd stared at Kevin long enough to make him sweat, sure. But when Kevin explained why he hadn't mentioned it sooner—his memory issues and that he hadn't been sure what he was looking at—Sam had just nodded. Said something about good instincts. Told him to trust his gut next time.

Kevin hadn't been able to shake that moment. Sam *trusted* him. Not a lot of people had. Not back then.

Now? Kevin felt like part of the team. Like he belonged here, in this rundown station with its creaky floors, stale coffee, and a cat with an attitude problem.

The phone on his desk buzzed, jolting him upright. He grabbed it. Sam.

"Yeah?"

"I'm done here," Sam said, his voice steady but clipped. "Heading to Marnie's. Meet me out front in ten."

The line clicked dead.

Kevin stared at the phone then at the clock. He was already moving, shoving his chair back and grabbing his jacket in one fluid motion. He was out on the sidewalk waiting when Sam pulled up.

CHAPTER FORTY-FOUR

The warm glow of Marnie Wilson's living room spilled faintly onto the cul-de-sac as Sam parked the cruiser at the curb. The modest colonial looked almost too picture-perfect—tidy flower beds, a pristine porch, and curtains drawn tight. Kevin adjusted his seat belt as Lucy shifted restlessly in the back.

"You ready?" Sam asked, his tone low.

Kevin nodded. "Let's see what she's hiding."

Sam stepped out. Lucy hopped out, too, her ears pricked as if sensing the tension. Sam glanced back at her. "Stay sharp, girl."

The doorbell chimed, its cheerful sound at odds with the gravity of their visit. Inside, the sound of hurried footsteps approached then hesitated. The door creaked open, revealing Marnie's cautious face.

"Chief Mason?" Her brows furrowed as she spotted Kevin and Lucy. "What's going on? It's late."

"Evening, Marnie," Sam said, his tone firm but polite. "We need to talk. It's important."

Marnie frowned, gripping the doorframe. "Can't this wait until morning? I have early meetings—"

"No, it can't," Sam interrupted, stepping forward enough to signal this wasn't a request. "This is serious."

Marnie hesitated then sighed, opening the door wider. "Fine. Come in."

The inside of the house was tidy, almost sterile, as if Marnie lived more for appearances than comfort. She motioned them toward the living room but remained standing herself, arms crossed defensively.

"What's this about?" she asked, her voice sharp.

Sam kept his tone measured. "We've been looking into Garvin McDaniels's murder, and your name keeps coming up."

Marnie laughed. "My name? That's ridiculous. Why would I have anything to do with that?"

"No idea. Beryl Thorne thinks you did," Sam said.

Marnie's eyes narrowed. "What do you mean?"

Sam kept his gaze steady. "She said you've been

interested in Garvin's property and that you're the one who made things happen."

Marnie stared at him, disbelief flickering across her face. "No," she said finally, her voice trembling. "No, Beryl wouldn't—" She stopped herself, her expression shifting as if the weight of something unspoken was pressing down on her. "She wouldn't say that."

"She did," Sam pressed, his voice calm but firm. "And she claims she has proof."

Marnie looked skeptical.

Kevin crossed his arms, his tone laced with skepticism. "She's protecting herself, Ms. Wilson. She doesn't care about you. If throwing you under the bus keeps her out of trouble, she'll do it in a heartbeat."

Marnie's eyes darted to Kevin then back to Sam.

"She's blaming you for this, Marnie. If you know something that can clear your name, you better speak up," Sam said.

Marnie hesitated, her breathing uneven. She looked away, her gaze fixed on some distant point on the floor. "I thought we were on the same side," she said quietly. "Beryl and I. She's been helping my campaign, supporting me. I thought..."

Sam stepped closer, his voice softening enough to edge past her walls. "You thought she had your back.

But she doesn't, Marnie. Not when it comes to saving herself. She'll pin it all on you and walk away clean."

Marnie swallowed hard, shaking her head. "She wouldn't do that. Not to me."

"She already has," Sam said. "She pointed the finger at you. Said you were the one pulling the strings."

Marnie's head snapped up, her face pale. "She said I was pulling the strings? That's not true. I'm not—" She cut herself off again, her eyes narrowing. "You're lying. Trying to get me to confess to something I had no part of."

"Blue paint, Marnie," Kevin said, his voice cutting through her excuses. "Same shade as your campaign posters. Found at Garvin's cabin. Care to explain that?"

Marnie's composure wavered. She opened her mouth, closed it again, then shook her head. "Anyone could've tracked that paint there. It doesn't mean anything."

Sam leaned in slightly, his voice quiet but firm. "We can tie it directly to you. You were there, Marnie. And if you keep denying it, you'll only make it worse."

Her breath hitched, and she stepped back, clutching the back of a chair for support. "This is insane. You're trying to railroad me—"

"No, we're trying to get the truth," Sam said, his voice rising enough to cut through her protests. "And here's the truth. If we take this to a jury, they'll see the evidence and convict you. When you're sitting in prison for murder, who's going to take care of your mother?"

The words hit like a hammer. Marnie froze, her face paling. Her hands trembled as she gripped the chair, her breath shallow. "What do you know about my mother?"

"I know about Parker Studies," Sam said.

"I didn't kill him," she said, her voice barely a whisper.

Sam didn't let up. "Then tell us who did."

Tears welled in her eyes, and she sank into the chair, shaking her head. "You don't understand. Beryl... She made me do it."

Kevin crouched slightly, his tone calm but insistent. "What did she make you do, Marnie?"

Marnie's chest rose and fell with uneven breaths. "Beryl wanted the property. She gave me money. I needed it for my mother. She told me to make sure Garvin sold the property to one of her shell companies. I just wanted to scare Garvin. To push him into selling. I didn't know—" Her voice broke, and she buried her face in her hands.

Kevin took a step forward, his tone steady but firm. "You didn't know what?"

"That it would go that far!" Marnie's head shot up, her eyes wet with tears. "I hired Desmond Griggs. He's... He's dangerous, but I didn't think he'd actually kill Garvin. I thought he'd pressure him, make him give up the property. That's all."

Sam exchanged a glance with Kevin, his mind racing. "When was this? Did you know Garvin was changing his will?"

Marnie shook her head vehemently. "No, I didn't even know about the will. I just... Beryl said we needed the property. She said it was important."

Sam narrowed his eyes. "Important how?"

"I don't know," Marnie admitted, her voice small. "She never told me why. Just that it had to be done."

Kevin crouched down slightly, leveling his gaze with hers. "What about Griggs? Has he contacted you since?"

"No," Marnie said, shaking her head. "I haven't heard from him. I don't know where he is."

Sam straightened, pulling his phone from his pocket. He sent a quick message to Wyatt, who was tailing Griggs, then turned his attention back to Marnie.

"Stay put," he said, his tone hard. "If Griggs

contacts you, call me immediately. And don't think about skipping town, Marnie. We're watching."

Marnie nodded weakly, her shoulders slumped in defeat. As Sam turned to leave, Lucy let out a soft growl, her ears flattening slightly. Sam reached down to scratch behind her ears, his jaw tight.

"You ready?" Kevin asked as they stepped back into the night air.

"More than ready," Sam replied. "Time to finish this."

CHAPTER FORTY-FIVE

S am parked the cruiser a block down from Griggs's house. Lucy shifted in the back seat, her ears perked, alert as always. Sam grabbed his flashlight and gun, motioning for Kevin and Lucy to follow.

Wyatt's unmarked car sat ahead, its silhouette blending into the quiet neighborhood.

Wyatt rolled his window down as they reached the car. "He's been inside for hours. Lights on, TV going. Looks like he's comfortable."

Sam glanced toward the small house, its curtains drawn tight, shadows flickering from the television's glow. It wasn't much—a sagging roof, peeling paint, a porch that looked ready to collapse—but inside was Desmond Griggs, their key to unraveling the tangled web around Garvin McDaniels's murder.

"Here's the plan," Sam said, his voice low. "I'll go to the front. Wyatt, you take the back. Kevin, cover that door on the side. Lucy stays with me."

Wyatt grinned. "You got it, boss."

Kevin nodded, gripping his flashlight.

They moved in silence, splitting off to their positions. Sam approached the front door cautiously, Lucy at his side, her ears swiveling to every sound. The door was locked, as expected. Sam leaned closer, listening for movement inside. The muffled sounds of an action movie filtered through, explosions and gunfire masking their approach.

He gave a subtle nod to Kevin, stationed by the side. Sam turned back to the door and knocked sharply.

"Desmond Griggs," he called, his voice firm. "White Rock Police. Open up."

Inside, the sounds of the TV abruptly stopped. Sam's hand tightened on his gun. Lucy let out a low growl, her stance shifting as she prepared for action.

Wyatt's voice crackled softly through Sam's earpiece. "He's moving. Back of the house. Looks like he's grabbing something."

Sam knocked again, louder this time. "Griggs! We know you're in there. Open the door!"

A beat of silence passed, then the lights inside went out.

"Move in!" Sam barked into his mic.

Wyatt surged toward the back door, Kevin covering the side. Sam kicked the front door hard, the frame splintering as it burst open. Lucy shot ahead of him, her growl echoing through the small, cluttered house.

"Police!" Sam shouted, sweeping his flashlight across the room.

Griggs was already bolting through the kitchen, a bronze statue of an elk tucked under his arm. He turned briefly, a glint of metal in his hand—a gun.

Sam ducked as Griggs fired, the shot slamming into the doorframe behind him.

"Lucy, go!" Sam commanded.

Lucy launched herself forward, her powerful frame hitting Griggs as he aimed again. Her teeth clamped onto his arm, forcing him to drop the gun with a clatter. Griggs roared in pain, twisting violently as he tried to shake her off.

Sam rushed forward, but Griggs managed to throw Lucy off, the dog landing hard but springing back to her feet with a snarl.

Griggs made for the back door, statue still in hand.

"Wyatt, he's coming your way!" Sam shouted.

The back door burst open as Griggs barreled through, colliding with Wyatt. They hit the ground hard, rolling in the dirt. Griggs swung the heavy statue, striking Wyatt's shoulder. Wyatt grunted, trying to wrestle the weapon away.

Sam and Kevin sprinted out after them. Lucy was right behind, her growls filling the air.

"Get off me!" Griggs snarled, raising the statue for another swing.

"Don't even think about it!" Sam bellowed, his gun trained on Griggs.

Griggs froze, his chest heaving, the statue poised in his hands.

"Drop it," Sam ordered, his voice ice-cold.

Griggs hesitated, his eyes darting between Sam's gun and Wyatt beneath him.

"Now!"

With a growl of frustration, Griggs let the statue fall to the ground. Wyatt shoved him off, scrambling to his feet with a glare that could've melted steel.

Kevin darted forward, kicking the gun away and cuffing Griggs as Sam kept his weapon trained on him.

Lucy circled Griggs, her tail high, her growl low and menacing.

Griggs sneered, blood dripping from the bite marks

on his arm. "You don't know what you're messing with," he spat.

Sam stepped closer, his eyes locked on Griggs. "Oh, I think we do. You killed Garvin McDaniels. You thought you'd get away with it, but you were wrong."

Griggs glared, his chest heaving.

Wyatt dusted himself off, wincing as he rolled his shoulder. "You hit like a wimp," he muttered, tightening the cuffs on Griggs.

Kevin picked up the bronze elk statue, examining it. "This thing matches the murder weapon perfectly." He looked at Griggs. "What, you thought you'd pawn it later once things cooled down?"

Griggs stayed silent, his eyes burning with fury.

Sam crouched slightly, meeting Griggs's glare head-on. "You're going to tell us everything. Who hired you, why you did it, and what you know about Garvin's land. Or you can rot in a cell for the rest of your life. Your call."

Griggs's jaw tightened, but he said nothing.

Sam straightened, holstering his weapon. "Let's get him out of here. We'll see how long he keeps quiet."

Wyatt yanked Griggs to his feet, his grip iron tight. Kevin followed with the statue, his expression grim.

Lucy stayed close to Sam as they headed toward the cruiser, her tail wagging slightly, her job done.

But Sam's mind was already racing ahead. They had Griggs, and the evidence was mounting. But there was someone higher up that had orchestrated this. Someone higher than Beryl Thorne even. Hopefully, Griggs would tell them who it was. Otherwise, they might never know the truth of who was really behind this and why they wanted that land so much.

CHAPTER FORTY-SIX

The glow of the television cast flickering light across Sam's office as he leaned back in his chair, arms crossed, watching Marnie Wilson's live press conference. Jo sat on the edge of the desk, arms resting on her knees, her badge clipped to her belt—a silent reminder of her reinstatement.

Marnie stood at a lectern, the White Rock mayoral seal prominently displayed behind her. Her face was pale, drawn tight with the weight of the decision she was being forced to make. She gripped the edges of the podium as though it was the only thing keeping her upright.

"After careful consideration, I have decided to withdraw from the mayoral race," Marnie announced, her voice steady but brittle. "This has not been an easy decision, but due to personal family matters, I must focus my attention where it's needed most."

Jo snorted softly. "Family matters. Sure, that's the reason."

Sam's eyes didn't leave the screen. "Her people wrote that for her. Probably took them hours to get the tone just right."

Marnie continued, forcing a smile that didn't reach her eyes. "I want to thank my supporters for their unwavering dedication and passion. White Rock deserves a leader who can give one hundred percent to this community, and at this time, I cannot do that."

"She's trying to salvage her reputation," Jo said, shaking her head. "But let's face it—her career's over."

Sam finally glanced at Jo. "That's the deal. She bows out gracefully and no charges are pressed. It's a win for her people."

"And a win for the rest of us too," Jo muttered. "Jamison might not be the best mayor, but at least he's not shady like Marnie."

On the screen, Marnie stepped back from the podium as reporters shouted questions, microphones thrust toward her. She didn't answer a single one, disappearing behind the curtain with the efficiency of someone who'd practiced the exit a dozen times.

Sam muted the television and rubbed his jaw. "She

got off easy. But you saw her back there—she's finished. She won't recover from this."

Jo stood, pacing the small office. "And Beryl? She just walks away too?"

"She was smart. Didn't leave any evidence pointing to her." Sam leaned forward, resting his elbows on his knees. "At least I've got leverage now. That photo in the box? It levels the playing field. Beryl won't risk using what she has on me, not if she knows I can hit back just as hard."

Jo stopped pacing, her expression hard. "It's not enough. She's still in the game. Still pulling strings."

"Yeah," Sam admitted. "But for now, she's neutralized. That's the best we can hope for."

Jo didn't look convinced, but she didn't argue. Instead, she turned toward the door. "I'm heading out. Got a meeting with Garvin's kids. Signing the Purchase and Sale for the cottage tonight."

Sam nodded. "Good luck."

She offered him a small, genuine smile. "Thanks, Sam. For everything."

As Jo left, Sam turned the volume back up, the muted hum of reporters filling the room. He leaned back, staring at the screen but not really seeing it.

Marnie was out of the picture. Beryl was temporarily contained. But Griggs's silence haunted him. Someone powerful and ruthless was still out there, pulling strings, and Sam didn't like how close they'd come to losing control of the game.

THE WARM GLOW of the fireplace flickered across the room, painting the walls of Jo's cottage with a golden light. Outside, the snow whispered against the windows, a muffled backdrop to the low hum of voices and laughter inside.

Jo stood near the kitchen, leaning against the counter, her eyes sweeping the room. Kevin was setting snacks on the coffee table. Beside him, Bridget was laying out plates, her movements practiced and efficient. Every now and then, their shoulders would brush, and Kevin would glance at her, quickly looking away before Bridget noticed.

Except she noticed. Jo could see it in the small, satisfied smile Bridget gave when she thought no one was looking.

In the corner, Mick was nursing a whiskey, one arm draped casually over the back of his chair. Lucy had claimed the rug in front of the fireplace, her head resting on her paws but her eyes flicking to each person in turn, her ears perking up at the occasional clink of glass or burst of laughter.

Wyatt was slouched in the armchair by the window, one boot resting on his knee, spinning a bottle cap between his fingers like he didn't have a care in the world. Except when he was checking his phone, which he seemed to be doing quite regularly.

Sam leaned against the mantel, his gaze flickering over the room, but Jo could tell he wasn't entirely at ease. He never was.

This was it, Jo thought. Her people. Her home.

Jo rose to her feet, lifting her glass in one hand and motioning for quiet with the other. The room settled, the hum of conversation fading as everyone turned their attention to her. She glanced around, meeting the eyes of each person present, her gaze lingering a little longer on Sam then Mick before finally settling on Bridget.

"I just wanted to say thank you," Jo began, her voice steady but warm. "Thank you for helping me get my badge back and for finding Garvin's killer."

She paused, letting the words hang in the air. It wasn't just gratitude she felt but relief—a deep, unspoken weight finally lifted from her shoulders.

"Griggs may not be talking," she continued, her tone hardening slightly, "but we've got the murder weapon. That's evidence enough to close the book on this part of the case. And none of it would've happened if it weren't for all of you."

Her gaze shifted to Mick, a faint smile tugging at the corners of her lips. "And Mick, I owe you a special thank-you. You stepped in when I was suspended and made sure I didn't lose my mind sitting on the sidelines."

Mick leaned back in his chair, a smirk playing on his face. "You're welcome, Harris. But in case you didn't notice, I didn't do much helping. You're so damn stubborn, you didn't let me."

A ripple of laughter moved through the room, breaking the tension. Jo rolled her eyes, but she couldn't help the grin that followed. "Seriously, though. Thank you—all of you. For having my back. For being here. It means everything to me."

Bridget disappeared into the kitchen, Kevin trailing after her. Jo watched them for a moment then wandered over to the fireplace where Sam was still leaning, his expression unreadable.

"Not bad for a little place in the woods," he said, his voice low.

"It's perfect," Jo replied, her gaze following Kevin and Bridget as they worked together in the kitchen.

Sam followed her gaze, one eyebrow quirking up. "Think those two are finally going to figure it out?"

Jo smirked. "Who knows."

The sound of a knock on the door pulled Jo's attention.

"I'll get it," she said, moving toward the door.

Before she reached it, the door creaked open, and Reese stepped inside, her cheeks flushed from the cold.

"Sorry I'm late," Reese said, brushing snow off her coat. "I got caught up at the station—"

Before she could finish, a blur of orange darted past her legs.

"Pickles!" Jo exclaimed as the cat bolted into the room, tail high and confident.

The entire room turned to watch as Pickles leaped onto the couch, circling once before curling into a ball like he owned the place.

"Well," Sam said, his voice dry, "looks like someone's finally decided to come inside."

Jo shook her head, a laugh bubbling out of her. "Took him long enough."

Bridget appeared in the doorway to the kitchen, her expression softening as she watched Pickles settle in. "Guess he knows this place can really be his."

As the laughter and conversation picked up again, Jo stood by the door, taking it all in. This wasn't just a house anymore. It was a home. And for the first time in what felt like forever, she knew she was exactly where she was meant to be.

Lucy padded over and nudged her hand, and Jo scratched behind her ears. "We did it, girl," she said softly. "We finally did it."

———

WYATT LEANED back in his chair, nursing his beer and letting the warmth of the room settle over him. The soft murmur of conversation and the occasional burst of laughter reminded him of something he hadn't felt in a long time: belonging. He glanced around the cozy space—Jo's smile as she stroked that oddball cat, Kevin and Bridget standing a little closer than necessary by the kitchen, Sam and Reese swapping dry remarks by the fire.

They'd included him, and it felt good. Because of his past, always moving, it was hard for him to make friends, and he wasn't used to being included.

Wyatt still wasn't sure how he'd ended up here, but he wasn't about to ruin the moment by overthinking it.

His phone buzzed on the cushion beside him. He hesitated. Checking it felt rude, like breaking the unspoken rule of the night—no work, no worries, just this fragile sense of normalcy. But it could be important.

The screen lit up with a message from his mom.

I'm okay. Nothing to worry about.

Relief washed over him. She'd been through enough. Her being okay was all that mattered. He was about to set the phone down when the second message came through.

Keep your eyes open. Your father might have found you.

His stomach dropped.

Wyatt stared at the screen, the words blurring slightly as the firelight flickered against it. He wanted to dismiss it, convince himself she was just being overly cautious. But his mom didn't send messages like that lightly.

He glanced up, forcing himself to look at the others. Kevin was laughing at something Bridget said, his face lighting up in a way Wyatt rarely saw. Jo looked at peace for the first time in months, the tension finally easing from her shoulders. Sam was sitting in the chair next to the fireplace, scratching Lucy behind the ears, his expression thoughtful but calm.

Wyatt wanted to stay in this moment, to let it wrap around him like a safety net. But the message on his phone whispered to him, pulling at the edges of his thoughts.

His father. The man they'd escaped all those years ago. If he'd found them...

Wyatt's jaw tightened, and he shoved the phone into his pocket, willing the bad feeling away. He didn't want to ruin this. Not now.

But as he watched the firelight play against the walls of Jo's cottage, he couldn't shake the thought that something in his life was about to change—and not for the better.

ALSO BY L. A. DOBBS

Sam Mason Mysteries

***

Telling Lies (*Book 1*)

Keeping Secrets (*Book 2*)

Exposing Truths (*Book 3*)

Betraying Trust (*Book 4*)

Killing Dreams (*Book 5*)

Crossing Lines (*Book 6*)

Seeking Justice (*Book 7*)

Breaking Rules (*Book 8*)

More books in the Rockford Security Series:

One Lie Too Many

Blink Of An Eye

Cold As Her Heart

A Game of Kill

No One To Trust

No Time To Run

Don't Fear The Truth

Hide From The Past

Liars Island Suspense Novellas:

***

Liars Lane

ABOUT THE AUTHOR

L. A. Dobbs also writes light mysteries as USA Today Bestselling author Leighann Dobbs. Lee has had a passion for reading since she was old enough to hold a book, but she didn't put pen to paper until much later in life. After a twenty-year career as a software engineer, she realized you can't make a living reading books, so she tried her hand at writing them and discovered she had a passion for that, too! She lives in New Hampshire with her husband, Bruce, their trusty Chihuahua mix, Mojo, and beautiful rescue cat, Kitty.

Her book "Dead Wrong" won the "Best Mystery Romance" award at the 2014 Indie Romance Convention.

Her book "Ghostly Paws" was the 2015 Chanticleer Mystery & Mayhem First Place category winner in the Animal Mystery category.

Join her VIP Readers group on Facebook:
https://www.facebook.com/groups/ldobbsreaders

Find out about her L. A. Dobbs Mysteries at:
http://www.ladobbs.com

Made in United States
North Haven, CT
28 February 2025

66322031R00167